THE THEATRE OF MAGIC
AND OTHER STORIES

RAFAEL COSENTINO

Copyright © 2024 Rafael Cosentino All rights reserved

The stories, characters, names, settings and events portrayed in this book are fictitious. Any similarity to real persons, living or dead, is coincidental and not intended by the author.

No part of this book may be reproduced, or stored in a retrieval system, or transmitted in any form or by any means, electronic, mechanical, photocopying, recording, or otherwise, without express written permission of the publisher.

ISBN: 9798875634543

Printed in the United States of America.

CONTENTS

	Introduction	i
1	Summer Triangle	9
2	That Clicking Noise	33
3	The Fountain	56
4	Rules Are Rules	67
5	Cassidy Got Lucky	88
6	The Theatre of Magic	117

INTRODUCTION

Ralph Waldo Emerson wrote, "The mind, once stretched by a new idea, never returns to its original dimensions." In many ways, stories are containers for ideas that stretch the mind. This collection is about many things: how we landed in the different chapters of our lives, the surreal situations we find ourselves in, and the fates we've narrowly escaped. I hope you'll allow these ideas to stretch your mind, too.

The Theatre of Magic

Summer Triangle

Our house was held together by decades of plaster patchwork and rental paint underneath years of cigarette smoke. It was a less-than-modest dwelling, but that's what Mom could afford. Even though our home felt like the lowest place on Earth, I'd always lifted my eyes to the stars, but staying optimistic was tough. Within these walls, there was no statute of limitations on shattered dreams, and you could hear the cries of broken lives groaning with the clogged pipes and growling air ducts. The carpet was an inky shade of defeat that absorbed hope like a black hole. Even with the windows open and the sunshine flooding in, the sensation of being trapped was inescapable. Mom and I had lived there for almost three years. I have no future in this town; that was Mom's mantra. You're on the road to nowhere, she reminded me daily. You get too attached, she'd scold. Hearing this non-stop irritated me, and I'd find excuses to leave. The thing is, I didn't have anywhere important to be.

It was the summer, so I drove to the Dunes, where I knew my only friend would be. It was Friday and 103 degrees. We stacked railroad ties in a square. The stack was six feet high when we ran out of wood. Carlos uncaped a gas can and doused the pile. The rising fumes blurred the views of the Franklin Mountains in the background. It was like seeing a mirage in the desert, and that's precisely where we were.

"It's just going to evaporate," I tell him, but he doesn't listen. He keeps pouring, and the dingbat has a lit ciggy dangling from his mouth. The kid was as dumb as a bag of hammers. I kept quiet, though, half hoping the pile would ignite, to watch him run around the dune on fire. I saw the tip of his cigarette blowing in the wind and felt a smile creeping up my jaw. The anticipation was splendid, but he finished pouring without ignition. In their generosity, the gods had allowed El Stupido to live another day.

I crack open a Dr. Pepper and sit under the only tree in sight. The Dunes are squarely in the middle of nowhere, about 200 yards from the Texas, New Mexico, and Mexico border. It's beautiful, really. The wind forms ripples in the sand, and it's quiet - nobody bothers us. We make fires, drink beer, and listen to music. There's a hill on one side called The Run where you can watch jeeps and 4x4s try to reach the top. The border patrol leaves us alone; they're too busy rolling out the welcome wagon for illegals.

So, I'm watching Carlos' gasoline evaporate when a Wagoneer pulls up. It parks, and these two girls hop out. The first was a stocky brunette wearing acid-wash jeans and a pink bikini top. I've seen her around. Her face was round, and her neck was too thick for her head. It looked like she was having a bad medical reaction. But it was Big Neck's friend that piqued my interest.

This girl's hair was Goldilox blonde, not too long, and it bounced as she moved. It was pushed up, maybe tied in the back, and a bunch fell on her shoulders, sun-kissed like her stomach. I could see a pink sunburn under her eyes and on her cute little nose, leading down to a pair of delicious pink lips. Her neck was thin but firm, and her collarbones were these magnificent sun dials showing off symmetry and youth. Two little white lines ran across either shoulder where straps had been, maybe yesterday or the day before. As I moved down, I took in her ample breasts, which didn't need any help from a little tube top, just barely hanging on.

She walked closer in these tiny jean shorts, and everything bounced just right. The fire alarm went off when I saw her eyes. They were treasure chests filled with turquoise and diamonds that sparkled in god's bathtub, and I froze up when she looked in my direction. Without overstating the moment, she was as glorious a creature as I'd ever seen.

The pair were a couple years older, maybe seventeen. They strolled over to Carlos and started asking about the bonfire. What time, who's coming, what should they bring and all that. Carlos answered their questions without even looking up. El Stupido is still conjuring mirages at 86 cents a gallon. He wasn't wearing a shirt, and they were checking him out. He had a fantastic build and beautiful brown skin; that was my friend, the Mexican Lion. But he's not introducing me or asking their names. The stars must have been aligned because the blonde looks over and smiles. God was throwing me a lifeline. Her look shot a lightning bolt down the back of my legs. I grinned right back only because I was paralyzed and couldn't do much else.

"Hi, I'm Enna," she says in a voice I can only describe as sultry. It wasn't girlie; it was older, and a slight raspiness held it together. Now Carlos is staring. "Hi Enna, I'm Alex," I say, nearly trembling. Carlos snickers, but Enna is still smiling. The 4 of us talk for a minute about the bonfire, and then Big Neck tells us they'll be back tonight. Then, the two returned to the Wagoneer and drove off.

It must have been after nine that night when I saw her again. Now, there were dozens of kids everywhere, mostly older. I was pumping air into the keg. Suddenly, I see Enna appear near the edge of the bonfire. I don't look up and feel panic build in my chest as she moves closer. I catch her looking around, so I rummage through a plastic bag and hand her a cup. "Thanks, Alex," she says in that delicious voice. Even though it's only been a few hours, she remembered my name. I play it cool, but I can't stop smiling. "Sure", I reply. "It's Enna. Am I saying that, right?" I ask. She nods enthusiastically, which quickly devolves into awkward silence.

So I was standing there blowing it when she asked where I went to school. A siren immediately roars because that question leads to your class, then your age. I was filling her cup and had to think fast. "Oh, I dropped out of high school to pursue a career in keg management," I say. I do a little action pose with the keg pump, and she giggles as I hand over the beer. A little foam dripped on her wrist, and I apologized for the heavy pour.

"You have beautiful eyes," she says to me. Now, I'm feeling enthusiastic. "Thank you, Enna; I was about to make the same observation; I do have beautiful eyes," I say. We both giggle. "No, but seriously, you have stunning eyes," I say. She laughs and then bats her eyelashes playfully. "Tell me more about my eyes," she whimpers like that momma bear in Bugs Bunny. I started laughing; she was laughing, we were laughing. This was great. "I've not seen you around," I say. "I've only been here a couple of times," she admits, and I can see her looking around the dune.

I thought she might walk away. "Have you seen the view from the top of the hill," I ask. Enna shakes her head. I point and ask if she wants to look with me, but she takes a minute to ponder the question. She studies my face and gives me the once over. "I'm not a serial killer, just a serious kegger," I say, but it sounded better before it came out of my mouth. The stars must have been aligned because she started giggling and smiling, which shot me right into orbit. "Sure, let's check it out," she says. I could see Carlos staring at us, and he was scowling, but I ignored him.

As we walked up the hill, Enna told me it was her first summer here, and she didn't know many people. She tells me about her parents and that they moved her for her dad's job. We're almost up the hill, but we stop and look back. Carlos' bonfire was practically an inferno now. The flames are so high you can probably see them from the highway. The whole dune was glowing orange, and the music from all the cars garbled together. There must have been fifty kids down there, and a few were dancing.

When we reached the top, she gushed about the view. "All those lights are in Mexico," I say, motioning toward the right. She beamed momentarily, sat down, sat back in the sand, placed her arms by her side, and then peered into the sky as if she could make sense of it all. So I sat back and looked up, too. The night sky was clear and bright. "Vega, Vega, Vega," she says slowly, then points. My eyes run up her arm, past her wrist, and slide against her beautiful finger until I spot it. Then she moved her finger down a bit. "That's Deneb over there, and a little lower and to the right, that's Altair. All three make up the Summer Triangle."

I didn't know anyone who could point out stars. "I'm genuinely impressed," I say. "I don't know much about stars or constellations, but it's fascinating." I keep looking up, and an awkward silence starts creeping in. "It's not a constellation," she says, turning her perfect face to mine. I've never been so overjoyed to be corrected. "It's an asterism," she mouths with elevated pronunciation. Then she stares at me with those giant green marbles. "Say it," she demands playfully and pokes me in the stomach. "As-ter-is-m," I repeat like a hypnotized zombie. "Very good," she giggles, feeling in command.

"The Summer Triangle is made of three bright stars from three different constellations." She uses her hands as she speaks, and I noticed the back of her arms are whiter than the Sunkist tops. "I'll bet you regret dropping out of high school now," she says as I'm ogling her ears and a heart-shaped earring that reflects the Moonlight. "I haven't really dropped out," I admit. "Typing class, wood shop, getting stoned in the parking lot, none of it feels like the future."

She cocks her head to one side like she's seeing me for the first time. "You're too good for school, then?" she asks. "Not at all. If only they taught cosmetology", I say while gliding my hand across the sky. We both giggle. "Learning about asterisms is more enlightening than getting stuck with my hands on the home row." I could tell she didn't understand, so I placed my hands on an imaginary typewriter. "F F F, JJJ," I say in the same zombie voice, pushing my pointers down. "Oh, for sure, typing is a total waste of time - they'll have computers to do that," she replies, staring up. "I don't think I'll forget this lesson," I say, and she looks at me again. "The teacher smells good, and the view is glorious." I didn't take my eyes away either; I couldn't. Enna's smile grew wide enough that I could see her teeth, perfect specimens. As the starring contest went on, her smile grew, as did mine, until we began laughing again.

I could sense she was comfortable, which put me at ease. "Please continue the lesson," I say and look up again. "OK, Vega appears as the brightest star in the constellation Lyra and is shaped like a harp." Now I'm staring into heaven and hanging on her every word. "Deneb is the brightest and most dazzling star in the constellation Cygnus the Swan. And Altair is the brightest star in the constellation Aquila the Eagle." I start wondering what older guys would say. "Which star is the closest," I ask. "Altair", she replies confidently. I wondered who was teaching her this stuff. She was so much more intelligent than girls I knew.

I immediately stood up. I had to. "Do you want another beer?" I ask nervously. "I sure do!" I grab her cup and run down the hill to fetch a couple more. Carlos seems annoyed. He asks me what I'm doing up there and if I'm coming down. I ignore him, fill the cups, and run back.

I fall back into my spot without appearing overly enthusiastic, and she takes the beer. "The question is," she says, holding a dramatic pause. Now I'm thinking she's about to ask my age. Hey, it was fun while it lasted. "Do you have a girlfriend?" she asks awkwardly. That turned me on like a light switch. And for a moment, I was paralyzed. "No, do you?" I asked nervously, without intending it to be funny, and she erupted in laughter again. We settled into a rhythm and talked about stars, parents, music, and love. We shut out everything else, and the rest of the world ceased to exist. It was just Enna and me underneath the Summer Triangle.

Toward the night's end, Enna turned and faced me head-on. I remember moving a little closer but stopping short. She leaned in and closed the distance until our mouths touched. We kissed. It was just a medium peck, then another until her lips parted, and she pushed her tongue inside my mouth. She tasted like watermelon bubblegum and beer. Her lips were soft. I smelled her suntan lotion. It was a sweet pineapple and coconut scent that was electrifying. Our hands touched lightly, and I moved my fingers over her wrists and arms. She made this little whimpering noise. I felt the back of her head and kissed her neck, but I was slow and kept my distance if you know what I mean.

The stars must have been aligned because she rolled closer and got on top of me. Now, she was straddling me, and I was looking at Enna's angelic face. She was staring down at me and surrounded by stars. Her legs fell to my sides, and she pushed her crotch into mine. Her hair was hanging down on one side, and her breathing was heavy. She felt incredible, but I was a little out of my element. You might assume my shock was inexperience, but I've been straddled once or twice. She moved her face down to me, and we kissed again. We held each other. She allowed her weight to rest on me; it was heaven on Earth. We touched, smooched, and talked a little longer, and then it was over.

We were walking down the hill, and there were less cars below. The fire was almost burnt out, just flaming ash now. I watched bright orange embers float into the sky. Enna grabbed my hand. "Do you like swimming?" she asked. "I love swimming," I say, even though I didn't. Enna tells me they have a pool and invites me to her house the next day. I didn't know anyone with a pool. "Be there around noon," she orders. I must have repeated the address in my head twenty times: 409 Pocono Lane, off Shadow Mountain. We said goodbye. She kissed my cheek and smiled. "Goodnight," I said.

On the ride home, Carlos was unusually quiet. I wait for him to ask about the night, but he stays silent, and I can tell something is eating him. El Stupido was never one to revel in my happiness. I was poor, uncultured, and destined for mediocrity. That put him at ease. Yes, I was naive, ignorant, and had no direction. My mother gave me zero guidance, so everything I knew came from public school and friends - can you imagine any better advice? It was 1986; I was in West Texas and learning how to use a typewriter. I couldn't have known how much trouble I was being prepared for, but I sensed it.

Carlos's parents were still married. He had a beautiful home, they had money, and he was going to college. In our friendship, he always had the upper hand. What bothered him tonight was the coconut and pineapple scent on my clothes. It lingered in the car exquisitely. I saw him try to ignore it. He played it calm for a few minutes but finally rolled the window down. The car filled with hot night air. When he finally rolled it back up, the smell was gone. That made him feel better. He inhaled deeply and let it out again. "Ahhh."

I woke to the sunlight passing through my bedroom window. I stared at the plaster on the ceiling long enough to notice the pattern. You can spot the shoddy quality best in the morning because the sun casts elongated shadows on the popcorn spackle. The shadows spread across the ceiling, forming a giant maze, but only for about 2 minutes each morning. My eye finds the path from the window above, through the shadowed labyrinth, to my closet on the other side of the room. One of the closet doors is broken and hanging off the slider.

I rummaged through the closet and picked out a yellow Corona tank top but changed my mind and tossed it back. I didn't want her parents' first impression to be of some low-rent West Texas party boy. I chose a cowboy snap-up because the shirt's little metallic stripes matched my sunglasses. My mother yelled something from her recliner about me stealing her Winstons, but I took the car keys and left.

On the drive to Ennas, I felt insecurity bouncing

around. I'd spent so many waking moments feeling insecure that I'd grown accustomed to living that way. What made me most nervous was the idea that her parents might ask about my plans for the future. Parents always wanted to talk about that. They said stuff like the 90s are just around the corner. Computers will run everything. But I had a built-in response for interrogations of this sort, and it worked like a charm. I'd seen a documentary about a man whose company built ships in Norfolk, Virginia. He had dozens of employees and was well respected. I adopted that cover story for situations like today. I'd tell them about my dad's shipbuilding business in Norfolk. Of course, it was a lie, but they usually stopped asking questions after hearing about it.

I found Enna's house, parked in front, knocked, and straightened my shirt and hair. The door opened, but it was just Enna wearing a blue bikini. I don't see her parents. I can't help but take inventory of her perfectly tan body. Now, her hair was down. There was this mischievous look on her face. "Hi," I say, staring into those giant green marbles. She pulls me into the house, kissing my cheek on the way in. We're walking through the house, and she's barefoot. I pick up the scent of her suntan lotion again. It was mixed up with perfume now, powerful, like a chemical. She hasn't said anything yet. We passed through the kitchen to a sliding glass door and ended up in a beautiful backyard. On the left, a glorious swimming pool stretched like a miniature ocean, and the water was glass. The surface was bright blue and reflected the sky.

I ever so innocently walked over to take a closer look, and would you believe me if I told you - Enna pushed me right in. Like a nervous hiccup, I laughed hysterically on the way down and kept laughing under the water. I took off my sopping shirt and tossed it on the edge. Enna jumped in after me, and within a minute, she held my hand underwater and pulled me closer. I could hardly believe it. She still hasn't spoken, but she's glowing now.

The way she moved on me, I struggled to get my bearings. "My parents are in Vegas for the weekend," she said reassuringly, and that set off the fire alarm. We kissed, and she pulled me against her. Her mouth was delicious. "I was thinking about you all night," she admitted. I'm dealing with wave after wave of shock, self-awareness, and euphoria, but I keep it together. We move through the water in each other's arms, mouths locked, touching, exploring.

After a few minutes, she said, "I want to show you something," then walked to the ladder and climbed out. She probably has one of those lamps that shines stars on the ceiling, so I follow her. We move through the house, wet and dripping over the living room carpet. It smelled like a stranger's house, not bad, just different. The walls are covered in a Western-style wallpaper that repeats over and over. I see cowboy hats, lassos, cactus, and boots. There were these little purple and yellow flowers, too.

She grabs my hand and stares at me like she's reading my mind. As we climbed the steps, I noticed her curves. I couldn't help but stare at that blue bikini bottom and imagine what might be underneath. She swayed back and forth up the steps, and something occurred to me: we were all alone. She parked me in the upstairs hallway and told me to wait. I stood there staring at those purple and yellow flowers on the wall.

After a moment, she spoke from inside the room. "OK, come in", she said. I twisted the knob, stepped in, and couldn't believe my eyes. Enna was lying on a bed completely naked except for a book she held in both hands, which covered her face but nothing else. The blue bikini sat balled up in the corner. Her room smelled like her perfume; it was sweet and light, like an island. "Take off your trunks," she said from behind the book. My heart was going now.

The situation was absurd. I could either run or do as I was instructed. I calmed myself and began pulling down my trunks. They were wet, so I loosened the string, and they came down OK. *Just breathe.* "Come-ere," Enna whispered. Cautiously, I inched closer, checking for loose floorboards, and was careful not to say anything stupid. She was lying there, so I let my eyes wander, and It was breathtaking. I knew what the parts looked like, but I'd never seen them laid out so entirely. I was no doctor, but her breasts appeared fully developed. Her skin was tan and smooth, even in the places the bikini had covered, just lighter.

I moved beside her, but still, she hid her face behind that book. She wouldn't have to admit what was happening if we didn't make eye contact. It was strange and perverted, but perhaps it was for the best, for both our sake. I don't remember the book's title, but without any warning, she took me into her hand, you know, down there. I froze up, but she was slow and gentle.

Enna knew things I didn't, and I was embarrassed about that. I wanted to look away, but I stared at what her hand was doing. Terrified but enthusiastic, I stood my ground and let her explore. Then she took my hand. "Lay on top of me," she ordered, still holding the book with her free hand. I did what she asked.

She spread her legs and guided me on top. I could smell her skin mixed with chlorine and sunshine. Her body was soft and warm. We kissed for a while, and then she motioned, so I pushed up from the bed so she could put me inside. She teased for a little. Her breathing was heavy, almost labored. Then she did it and pulled me closer. "Pump like this," she whispered in my ear. After a few moments, I was matching her rhythm. "That's nice," she said, exhaling the air from her lungs.

Enna pulled and touched me. I held and touched her. She was strong and in total control. I saw the little blonde hair on her perfectly tan skin. I could smell us and hoped Enna was enjoying it. Peering into those giant green marbles, I could see she was. I focused on her breathing. She made more of those little whimpering noises. The room became still - everything got slower. I heard the bed creaking, and we matched each other's motions until we'd found what we were looking for.

My mind was at peace on the drive home. After taking an inventory of my relatively short life, being with Enna had to be the best moment yet. I was drenched in her pineapple and coconut smell and imagined our lives together. I wondered what I'd be willing to do – what I'd have to do to make her happy. I fell in love with her on the drive home. I really did.

I had barely entered the front door, and Mom began criticizing me as usual. I didn't have a future here. I'd be better off with my father in Seattle. The high schools were better there, and he could help me find a job after graduation. We ate dinner, and Mom reminded me about her church choir performing Friday night. I had promised to go. After dinner, I began to ache. I had this urge to hear Enna's voice. I was obsessed, truly a madman. "Do you hear me"? Mom yelled. "Yes, I'm just thinking," I replied. Mom continued washing dishes. "I stopped trying with you, Alex." She continued. Her sermons were endless. "You live in your head; you think you know better than everyone else. The world can be a harsh teacher, but that's the only teacher that will get through your thick head. "Sorry, Mom," I said, trying to calm her. The woman was always disappointed.

Nothing could get me to leave now. I could hardly speak when I left Enna's house and had forgotten to get her number. I thought about calling information, but that felt desperate. There were still two months of summer left. Of course, she'd be at the Dunes again. I'd see her soon; no need to be clingy and scare her away.

Those green eyes and her scent, the way she held my hand and stared. And as corny as it sounds, I changed how I slept in bed. A small change can lead to a big one. I refused to look at that popcorn spackle. I switched my position so my head was on the other end. Now, I could peer out the window into the night sky. I'd find the Summer Triangle and imagine Enna lying beside me in the sand, smiling and pointing out asterisms.

The week was uneventful. I mostly did yard work for Mom and our neighbor, who gave me 20 dollars. Finally, it was Friday morning. I pulled into 7-11 and spotted Carlos in the parking lot. "Hey man, you going to the Dunes tonight?" I ask. "Ya, but Alex, I'm still pissed you blew me off last time." The idea that I'd blown him off was absurd. We'd spent the entire day together except for the night. "What, c'mon C, you're my Mexican lion, always," I tell him. "You're going to let a girl come between us?" I asked, and he smiled. "I'll be there for sure, but not till later. My mom is singing tonight, and I promised I'd go." He nodded. "You making a bonfire again?" I ask. "Nah, man, that's a big hassle," he says. "I bust my ass keeping the fire going, and all the girls get taken." He smiles, and I know we're OK. "I hear that", I reply. "See you tonight, C-man."

Mom's performance was beautiful. She dressed in an outfit she'd picked out at the downtown thrift store. Her choir friends cracked on her fashion, screaming she could only be described as a Southwest disco gypsy. They were hicks but good salt-of-the-earth folks. I found Mom's name in the program; she even had a short solo. I'd never seen the church so full, but I'd never been to church on a Friday night, so what did I know? She was beaming with excitement. When It was over, I gave her a big hug. I wondered if she could understand what was happening to me. She stared at me longer than usual. It was past ten, but I could reach the Dunes in twenty minutes.

When I arrived, I saw about 30 cars. I scanned around, and low and behold, there it was - Big Neck's Wagoneer. Enna had to be here, too. I drove past the big dune and parked by the hill. I walked up the dune and could hear music and laughter over the ridge. As the scene came into view, I saw a few kids sitting huddled by a small fire. As I moved closer, the music grew louder. I noticed familiar faces and could make out most of the usual suspects.

Then, right between some people standing, I spotted blonde hair on a girl sitting down - it was Enna. She was sitting in Carlos' lap. They were kissing and had their arms around each other. She wore the same blue bikini top. I could hardly process what I was seeing. I stopped walking and stood there completely still. This had to be a bad dream. *It can't be.* They were just playing a cruel trick on me. But there she was, straddling him. My heart sank into my stomach, and a knot formed in my neck.

Enna looked in my direction, and our eyes met, but just as fast, her eyes moved away. She'd taken Carlos in the spur of the moment, and Carlos was happy to fill in. Neither of them had given me a second thought. Self-awareness and inferiority filled my broken heart. I was nothing, no one. Instinctually, I turned away and returned to the car, tears streaming down my cheeks. I felt defeated, embarrassed, and too unworthy to confront them. Pressure welled up in my sinus. My hands were trembling. Seeing my hands shake as I tried to start the car was surreal. I calmed myself, drove home, went straight to my bedroom, and stared at the popcorn plaster until I passed out from exhaustion.

In the morning, I couldn't hold back the anger. I paced the house and then dialed Carlos. His dad answered and said he was sleeping. I began admitting to his dad that I was angry with his son and that the call was important. I told him that his son was a piece of shit. I couldn't believe the words coming out of my mouth. I was twisting the phone cord around my wrist and wondered if I should drive over and wrap it around C's throat. There was some static until I heard his voice. "Hello," he said smugly. His voice was tired; had Enna slept there, I wondered. "Hello," he spoke again. "Did you screw her" I demanded. There was just silence. "Did you screw her?" I asked again calmly. Finally, he spoke. "What, ahh man, you're all worked up."

I listened intently for clues as to why they would do something so cruel. "I saw you last night, C - you're a real piece of shit." There was more awkward silence. "Alex, she came onto me, bro; you know I love you." My vision throbbed. I was tired of feeling insecure, weary of this dwelling, the rental shag, the popcorn ceiling. I slammed the receiver down, and the little bell inside echoed throughout the house. "What the hell is going on!" my mom screamed from the living room. "Nothing!" I shouted back, channeling rage.

And in that instant, I realized that nothing was exactly what was going on. Absolutely nothing. I had nothing here. My mother meant well, but I was a sitting duck destined to follow in her footsteps. I could see my life laid out: low-wage jobs and rentals, layaway plans, and endless staring through the lens of hopelessness at tobacco-stained walls from a life relegated to a Barcalounger.

I steadied myself, then moved purposely to the living room with an anger-induced clarity I don't remember having before. I had to leave this place. I'd move to Seattle with my father. Although it was my only option, an option I'd dreaded, I was suddenly quite excited to walk the plank. I had no idea what awaited me there, but I didn't care, and that's exactly how I explained it to Mom. I was slow, focused, and determined.

She nodded and was supportive of my sudden change of heart. It was like she was expecting it. That was on Saturday morning. She immediately called my dad and made the travel arrangements. My bus left the next day, which was a Sunday. I remember because it was raining and it hardly ever rains in the summer.

That Clicking Noise

Dr. Lucas Bennett had been practicing psychiatry for over two decades, and in all his years of clinical work, he couldn't remember feeling more electrified than he did that Friday morning. After passing through base security, he walked through the sprawling military complex with a kick in his step. This was his 8th visit, an evaluation requested by the military for one of their own.

His patient, Army Specialist Emily Harris, was a woman whose resilience and strength he'd learned to admire over their previous sessions. The sun beat down on his face, and the West Texas heat carried the distant sounds of marching and orders being shouted as military vehicles drove past. As he walked towards the base detention center where they would meet, his mind wrestled with maintaining the delicate balance between his growing affection and his duty as a psychiatrist. Although it didn't happen often, he was emotionally invested in the case. He'd made a discovery that could transform his patient's life, which excited him profoundly. In fact, he'd be hard-pressed to cite another example of identifying the root cause of a patient's mental paralysis so precisely.

He'd spent the last few weeks investigating everything he'd learned from their sessions. He spoke to colleagues, performed extensive database research, and studied dozens of similar cases. A couple of nights ago, he stumbled upon an exact match. He was optimistic it would end her suffering, give her clarity, her life would change for the better, and she would be forever grateful. He was well-groomed today. His salt and pepper hair matched the pattern of his tortoiseshell glasses. His skin was tan and smooth, and he had a sharp nose, which made him look younger than he was. His hands were well-manicured. You'd notice them because his shirt sleeves were rolled up to just below his elbows. He walked past Echo Barracks and smiled, realizing he was the only person here not wearing fatigues.

As he entered the detention facility, a pair of stern-faced security personnel motioned for him to stop. They rifled through his bag with methodical indifference, their brusque manner grating against his nerves. The Doctor was permitted entrance into the detention center only after a burly MP patted him down. The Doctor was escorted down the usual hallway to the same sparsely furnished office where he waited for his patient to arrive. He sat down in the same beat-up red leather chair, which was finished with dozens of brass bullet nose tacks. A white noise machine hummed in the corner of the room.

After a few minutes, another MP stepped down the hallway, escorting a woman wearing a chocolate-brown prisoner uniform. She had medium-length black hair, and it shined in the fluorescent light. Her eyes were kind but defeated, and when he looked at her, he felt compelled to feel sorry for her. But neither pity nor mercy was part of his job. "Hello, Emily," the Doctor said as he greeted her. "Good morning, Lucas," she replied with a genuine smile. The MP uncuffed the woman and sat her in the chair on the other side of the steel desk. She took a deep breath and relaxed as if this was all routine, and it was. The office smelled like lemon cleanser and static electricity. The only sound was the hollow whoosh of the white noise machine humming away.

"It's so nice to see you," the Doctor said as he retrieved a laptop. He began moving his fingers across the keyboard. "How are you feeling?" he asked without looking up. "I think stable," she answered, staring at the Doctor's face, which was now illuminated, and the laptop's screen reflected on his glasses. "As usual, I will audio record this, OK?"

"Of course," she replied, studying the shape and color of his teeth. The Doctor pressed the button on a small tape recorder. "Today is Friday, June twentieth, two thousand and three. It's nine minutes after eleven am. This is Doctor Lucas Bennett, and I'm with Army Specialist Emily Harris at the Fort Bliss Detention Center." He fiddled with his laptop's touchpad, looking for the similar cases he'd discovered. He thought about an ideal way to structure this critical session, which he suspected might be their last.

"When I got your message about today's session, I began to feel hopeful," the woman said, breaking the silence. "I'm excited to know what you've learned." The Doctor looked up. "That's wonderful to hear, Emily. I believe you're ready to understand the root cause of your experiences. I mentioned that I have access to a national database of psychiatric cases. I don't always find relevant data that can be used to identify a patient's symptoms or accelerate their progress. Two days ago, I found something that matches your case more precisely than anything I've seen in my career. I was dumbfounded, to be totally honest." The woman's eyes lit up, and she shifted in her chair, staring at him, but her mind was reeling in anticipation.

"Here's what I think we should do," he continued. "First, I want to summarize everything we've discussed over the past 2 months. This review is critical for you. Then, I'd like to share what I've learned and how I believe it relates to what's happening to you. Is that OK with you?"

"Yes," the woman said through a forced grin. As he settled back into his chair, the Doctor breathed deeply. "OK, take me back to the first time you can remember hearing the clicking noise. Tell me where you were and what you experienced."

The women nodded, stared at the ceiling, and then spoke. "I was commuting to work on a bus as I always had. It was a Tuesday, and it was my mother's birthday." The Doctor stared without blinking. "I called her on my cell phone, and we spoke briefly. As my bus approached the city, I noticed a large hole in one of the twin towers. Black smoke was billowing out. I asked my mother to turn on CNN to see what happened, but she didn't see anything. Everyone on the bus was looking and pointing, and I knew something was terribly wrong.

We were much closer just a few minutes later as the bus rounded the bend to enter the Lincoln Tunnel. The whole bus was staring at the smoking tower across the Hudson River when I noticed a commercial airplane flying low and fast. It appeared to pass behind the towers, but I saw an explosion appear on the other side where the plane should have reappeared. The fireball moved up the side of the building. I heard people on the bus scream and gasp. An alarm went off in my mind, and I knew I had to record what I saw because I was witnessing something catastrophic. That's when I began to hear the clicking noise. I realized the noise was coming from inside my head, but it wouldn't stop. I watched the fireball rise over the towers and heard the other passengers screaming. The clicking noise continued for around thirty seconds as I processed what I saw and heard. I don't know what shocked me more: the plane crashing into the building, the realization people were dying, the screaming on the bus, or the clicking noise."

"You've said several times now that you had to record what you saw but didn't have a video camera, correct?"

"No, Lucas, I did not have a camera," his patient replied as if she'd answered the question a hundred times. "OK, and what does the clicking noise sound like?"

"Well, It's a little like one of those old reel-to-reel film projectors we had in grade school," the woman said as she made a turning motion with her hands and rolled her tongue on the top of her mouth, making a fast-clicking noise through her teeth. "tjj tjj tjj tjj tjj tjj."

The Doctor perked up. "Now we're getting somewhere, and Emily, when was the second time you heard the clicking noise?"

She pulled one leg under the other and made herself more comfortable. "It was the same day, about 30 minutes later", she replied. "When I got to work at Herald Square, the streets were frantic. It was pure chaos. People were yelling and trying to use their cell phones, but they weren't working. I heard sirens everywhere. In front of my office building, a colleague told me he was going home to get his pregnant wife. They lived just two blocks from the World Trade Center, across from Battery Park. I had to see what was happening and agreed to go with him, at least part of the way. There were police, fire trucks, ambulances, sirens, people running in every direction. We moved quickly down Ninth Avenue toward the smoking towers, and the closer we got, the worse things looked. We saw people crying, fire trucks, people screaming and running. It was a real horror show. By the time we made it to 18th Street, we could plainly see people falling from the towers. Their bodies seemed to tumble down the length of the buildings." The woman's eyes became teary, and her voice shook. The Doctor curled his lip. "Take your time", he said.

"We just stood there watching," she said through tears. "The people around us were watching this happen; many were crying, some were praying. An older woman standing in the Street next to me began to vomit uncontrollably, and I heard a jet plane in the sky moving closer. That's when the clicking noise started again. It was louder that time. I saw more bodies falling from the towers; they were dying, and the woman was vomiting. Just then, the jet plane streaked across the sky. It was a fighter jet. There must have been 100 people standing in the street, and I remember seeing the crowd turn their heads toward that fighter jet. I watched their faces move in unison as it streaked across the sky. The ground shook, and I could smell the woman's vomit. I recorded all that while the clicking noise played. I was frozen with fear."

My colleague told me that he thought I was having a seizure.

The Doctor's head jerked a little, but he straightened himself out. "OK, but again, you didn't have a camera with you, right Emily?"

"No, Lucas. It was a feeling I had, a sensation. I needed to record what I'd witnessed to prevent it from happening to others." The woman was not smiling anymore. Her face was at rest, almost falling. But something in her eyes was determined to hold on to the notion that the Doctor sitting across the desk could free her from the burden.

"And when was the third time you heard the clicking noise?" the Doctor asked, pushing his tortoiseshell glasses farther up on his nose. The woman rolled her head around her neck and spoke. "My cell phone finally started working, and I got a call from another friend who also worked in the city. The situation on the streets deteriorated; it was mayhem, and we had to leave immediately. They were evacuating people, and we agreed to meet at Chelsea Piers, where the ferry would take us across the Hudson to Hoboken." The Doctor handed the woman some tissues. She cleaned her eyes and blew her nose.

"While crossing the Hudson on the ferry, we saw the first tower collapse. It was almost right in front of us. I realized that the steel skyscraper I'd been inside so many times was crumbling. And I knew I was watching people die, maybe thousands. People on the ferry were crying, screaming out to god. And then another jet fighter streaked across the sky. That's when the clicking noise started playing again. I watched the people around me gasping and crying in horror. We watched this massive rolling debris cloud expand." The woman stopped momentarily to take a deep breath, but the Doctor motioned for her to continue.

"From Hoboken, they evacuated us to Giant's Stadium in New Jersey. From there we could see all of downtown. It was this huge ball of smoke and dust. You couldn't see the jets anymore, but we could hear them."

The Doctor moved his jaw back and forth to process his thoughts. "That was really something you witnessed. Every time you describe it, I can feel the gravity. And I can understand why it made a permanent impression in your mind's eye. So many people suffered terribly that day. When was the fourth time you heard the clicking noise?"

"The first three times happened that day, but the

fourth time happened 14 months later, now 4 months ago. I enlisted in the military a few weeks after 911. I felt compelled to prevent anything like that from happening again. A lot of people felt the same. After basic training, I was deployed to Afghanistan. My unit was assigned to the Tangi Valley. That's the Maidan-Wardak Province, a valley about twenty kilometers from Kabul. It's an ugly, dark place. I was already scared out of my mind, and the place looked like a nightmare. The valley is surrounded by these jagged, saw-toothed-looking mountains infested by insurgents."

The woman inspected the palms of her hands to see if they were shaking. "And those people don't care whether they live or die," she continued. "They're uneducated, violent, hate-filled religious fanatics teaming with small arms, RPGs, and IEDs. But they want to capture you alive so they can cut your head off. I got used to feeling scared, and time passed, lots of time. But four months ago, I was asked to join another unit that was collecting Intel on a suspected Taliban bunker located underneath a house. We drove to a small shanty village. Trash and clothes were blowing all over the streets. It was very windy, and I usually love the wind, but not that day. There were packs of wild dogs and sickly-looking people eating trash on the road. Everything was hard to look at."

The Doctor referenced a legal pad where he'd taken some notes. "A British soldier was speaking on the radio to confirm that he'd spotted a group of six Taliban soldiers. He confirmed they had light arms and RPGs, and we watched them walk inside the bunker house. I remember seeing a silver and gold Rolls-Royce pull up to the house."

"What about the car?" the Doctor asked, referring to his notes. "Seeing such an expensive car parked next to that metal shack was strange.", the woman replied. "Then we got an unusual call. One of the units confirmed that a man inside the house was a Taliban leader named Mullah Umar Maktomb, a high-value leadership target. We were asked to paint the house so air support could drop a JDAM."

"Our unit was behind a rock wall about a quarter mile away, and I asked to look through the spotter's binoculars. I could see movement in the house. I watched for a minute as we waited. As I heard the F18s overhead, I saw three children leave the house. And, they were laughing and smiling and holding hands."

The women's breathing became labored. Her abdomen quivered. She used the sleeve of her prisoner uniform to wipe the tears welling up in her eyes. The Doctor stood up and handed her some tissues. "It's OK, Emily, take your time," he said softly."

"I saw the children, but I knew it was too late to do anything, so I just watched. As the roar of the jets moved above us, the clicking noise started again, and it was louder than ever before. I watched those children get vaporized and realized we were the bad guys. I realized I was the bad guy. The clicking noise was still playing in my head when the bomb's shock wave hit us. I cried uncontrollably; that was the first time the clicking noise paralyzed me. I couldn't control myself. I curled into a ball. That's when the obsession started. Then, the clicking noise began playing when I was alone or watching TV. It would happen when I was eating, using the bathroom, anywhere. Each time I heard it, I was overcome with terror. It was happening 3 or 4 times a day. I began to fear it would happen every waking moment. I was paralyzed with terror."

The Doctor took off his glasses. "Emily, did you take money from the wreckage of the Rolls-Royce after the airstrike?"

"No, I didn't take any money. I didn't even know about that", she replied. "I don't remember the moments after the shock wave hit me. I was curled up in a ball."

The Doctor looked unconvinced. "As you know, the others in the operation claim they didn't see any children."

"Of course, they said that, "she shot back, shaking her head at the naive Doctor. "They told me to stop saying I saw children, and when I wouldn't, I became their enemy." The Doctor made notes on the same legal pad and then pointed at her with the pen. "And then there's this duffle bag that allegedly contained six million dollars," the Doctor continued. "A bribe intended for the Taliban leaders, or at least this is what your superiors tell me. Allegedly, the bag has still not been recovered. In addition to asking you, they tell me several others are under investigation."

"I took nothing," the woman screamed. "I don't care about money – I've told you that repeatedly!"

The Doctor replied quickly. "Then why did you steal Corporal Simon's passport? Why did you impersonate her? Why did you get on the C130 to London and then take a commercial flight back to the US? Where did you get the money to buy a $2,300 plane ticket to Newark?"

"I've answered those questions," she pleaded. "Emily," the Doctor roared, then calmed himself. "Tell me again."

The woman sniffled and pulled in a deep, cleansing breath. "I thought I was going crazy; my life had turned into a waking nightmare. I was always disoriented but kept it hidden from my superiors. I started hearing the clicking noise constantly. It was torture. I had to get out of there; I was a danger to myself and those around me. I had enough sense to take Simon's passport and the transport plane to London. My mother wired me the plane fare. You know the rest. They arrested me at the Newark airport; I had nothing but the clothes on my back. They charged me with desertion and impersonation. They didn't find any money, but if I had not been making noise about the murder of those children, do you think I would have been accused of stealing money?"

"I don't know", the Doctor replied.

"Have you seen any evidence that there was a bag of money?" she asked.

"No," he admitted after a moment. "Nor have I seen evidence that any children were killed in that operation."

Now, the women became quiet and still. The only sound was the humming of the white noise machine. The Doctor sat up in his chair and grabbed his laptop. "It's time for me to share what I've learned. This question may be strange, but I want you to take it at face value." The women nodded. "Emily, have you ever seen a movie called The Twilight Zone? It's not the original black-and-white series but a feature-length movie released in 1983. You might have been around ten years old when you saw it."

The women looked at the wall for the answer. "Yes, I do remember that movie," she replied. "Well, then, you know that the movie was a series of stories. Do you remember the story titled Nightmare at Twenty Thousand Feet? It takes place on a commercial flight. There's a monster on the wing; they're in a fierce thunderstorm..."

"Yes, I saw that. I do remember that", the woman said, cutting him off.

The Doctor's eyes lit up. "Tell me the scene; tell me what you remember about that story." He sat up straight in the chair enthusiastically.

"Well, like you said, they were flying through a horrible storm, and there was a strange creature on the plane's wing, and it was causing damage to the plane's engine. A passenger seated by the window saw what the creature was doing. He knew the creature would cause the plane to crash." The woman used her sleeve to wipe tears from her eyes.

"The passenger got hysterical, and the crew tried to calm him down, but he grabbed a gun strapped to the leg of an air marshal, and he shot out the window of the plane, trying to kill the creature. The cabin depressurizes, debris and passengers start flying around the cabin, and the plane goes into a nosedive."

The woman's eyes suddenly became very wide, as did the doctors. Her body became erect, as if she'd woken up.

"Yes, the jet's engines were roaring. The people in the cabin are screaming, and then a camera drops from the plane's ceiling and begins to record what's happening to the people inside." The woman clasped her hands together aggressively. "Jesus, of course. Like a projector, the camera that drops down shines light on everything it sees in the plane's cabin. It makes a clicking noise while it's recording. That's the noise, that's the clicking noise!"

The woman places her hands on her cheeks, and her stomach quivers. "How could you know this?" she asked excitedly.

"OK, stay with me, Emily! And what's the feeling you get when you think about that camera dropping from the ceiling to record everything?" He asks.

"It's too late to help anyone," the woman gasps. "They're all going to die, and the camera's only purpose now is to record their deaths."

"What does the camera do with the recording, Emily?"

"The camera sends what it sees to the plane's black box."

"Why does it do that, Emily?" the Doctor asks. "So when the wreckage is found, humanity can understand how they died." The Doctor nodded his head positively. "Exactly, Emily," he said softly. "In the psychiatric database, I found fourteen other cases that report associations between the events of September 11th and that scene in the movie Twilight Zone. Some people associate a sound or an idea with a movie. Still, unlike you, most of those patients made a conscious connection between the movie and the events of that terrible day. Because you never made the connection, it became an obsessive disorder. The other thing your mind may know is that while filming that movie, there was a scene where a helicopter malfunctioned and decapitated three actors, one adult and two children. Did you know that?"

The woman nodded, "Yes, I remember that. Many years ago, while in high school, I saw something on television about that accident and got a strange feeling about the movie. This is incredible. I can see where these ideas and the clicking noise came from." The Doctor smiled profoundly.

"I want to read you a transcript from a patient in one of the cases I found." The Doctor looked at his laptop and began reading. "I remember seeing the camera drop from the ceiling and becoming aware that even though those people were going to die, mankind needed to record what had gone wrong to prevent it from happening to others. I was a kid then, but that scene was my first realization that even while people were dying, mankind needed to record what was happening, which terrified me."

"That quote is precisely what you told me about the first time you heard the clicking noise, about your need to record it. But the quote is from a woman who lives in Virginia Beach. She's your exact age, too. What's interesting about this group phenomenon is that it's what psychiatrists call a psychosocial crisis or mass trauma. When smaller groups are affected by the same input, it's often called a cluster trauma. Each of the fourteen documented cases is about your age. That's not a coincidence, Emily? All fifteen of you saw that movie at a highly impressionable point in your mind's development, and it left a permanent mark." The woman shook her head in astonishment, and the

Doctor continued.

"That scene and the ideas presented are horrific for an adult but particularly impactful on young minds. I think about the 3 children you think you saw die and the 3 people killed on the film's set. I can't help but think there's a connection. Our mind's our incredible things. They take in things we don't think about consciously. Obsessing over those concepts can create a permanent fear in your subconscious mind. That's a little like the plane's black box, which records everything for future playback. The plane, the camera, the idea that you had to record people dying, the real helicopter accident on the film set. When you first heard the clicking noise, your mind's eye was just playing back the association because you saw a real plane hit that building, and what you were seeing was something that had gone horribly wrong."

The woman was calm but alert. "I really get it now," she offered the Doctor in a thankful tone. The woman breathed in and out several times very deliberately while she processed the realization.

"Now that you understand the association your mind created, you no longer have to be scared of the clicking noise. Emily, there's nothing wrong with your mind's black box. As a matter of fact, it's in prime working order. Your subconscious mind created a noise your conscious mind could hear. It scared you so much that the clicking noise became an obsession, and you panicked. That's how it became a disorder. Now you know the noise was something scary you saw in a movie as a kid. There is nothing wrong with you or your mind. Our minds are complex, and we must accept that we cannot control what gets recorded or when it gets played back."

"Does this mean I was justified in going AWOL?" the woman asked. The Doctor shrugged his shoulders. "That's not for me to decide Emily. I'm here to assess whether you had a psychotic break. Now that I've found the other cases, I can say with some certainty that something did break in your mind. When this happens, no one can know how the mind will react."

"Thank you, Lucas, for everything.", the woman said in a tone that brought the Doctor a deep sense of gratification. The two stood, smiled, and embraced for the first time in their eight weeks together. They stared into each other's eyes for a moment. They said their goodbyes and the Doctor was escorted out. The MP escorted the women down a long, fluorescent hallway.

Reaching the end of the hallway, the MP unlocked a door, and the women stepped back into the detention facility dormitory. She took in the moment, realizing the new beginning the Doctor had gifted. She walked to a payphone at the far end of the dormitory, picked up the receiver, and pushed some buttons. "Collect call from Emily." The operator made the connection. "Yes, I'll accept the charges," the voice on the other end replied. "Emily, how did your session go?"

"It just ended."

"Did the doctor make the association to the movie?" the voice asked. "Yes", the woman replied.

"Did you react the way we practiced?" the voice asked. "Yes, Dr. Bennet said exactly what you knew he'd say, and I reacted the way you taught me. It was like clockwork. I should be back in court next week. I suspect they'll release me the same day."

"Oh, Emily, this is incredible news," the voice said. "Listen closely; the judge may ask where you'll stay when they release you. Tell them you'll stay with me and that I'll get you the care you need. I've sent an affidavit to your lawyer. And, Emily, whatever you do, don't tell anyone that I'm a psychiatrist."

"I won't, Mom. Did you get the duffle bag from luggage storage at the airport?" The woman was biting her lips.

"I have it, Sweetpea, and it's incredible. This changes everything. We'll have to get you one of those money-counting machines. You know what they sound like, don't you?" the voice asked.

The woman looked around the jail dormitory then made a turning motion with her hands and rolled her tongue on the top of her mouth, making a fast-clicking noise through her teeth. "tjj tjj tjj tjj tjj tjj." The two women erupted in a burst of uncontrollable laughter.

The Fountain

A deep throbbing pain penetrated the marrow of his bones, and a pounding headache caused his vision to blur. Every step he took was agonizing, but the old man was strong and had grown accustomed to living with the pain. It was cancer spreading through his body, killing and replacing his healthy cells. He might have a chance if only his healthy cells could recognize the invaders. He pondered nature's method of making room for new people, which was relatively simple:

getting rid of the old ones. So it was ironic, he thought, that cancer cells are older cells that refuse to die. And because the mutated cells were his own, his immune system could not detect them as unfriendly.

As he walked, he thought about life's continuous cycle, birth and death, but the pain interrupted him. His mind was going, too. So many of his memories were just beyond his grasp, and he thought he'd rather die than go on in this pitiful state. He was sure all the people who had come and gone before him had decided to succumb to death rather than live this way. As he struggled down the narrow cobblestone street, he passed a small sidewalk café. A young woman noticed him and began speaking.

"Hello, signore," she said with a thick Italian accent. "It might be good to sit and relax for a while." Sensing his weakness, the young woman guided the dizzy man to a small table. He followed her lead and sat, allowing his weight to fall into the chair all at once. "Si, grazie," he said, huffing and puffing. She gave the man a once over, obviously concerned about his age and poor health. She could only smile and allow the man to catch his breath. "Thank you, signora," he puffed, and the woman pressed her lips together, wondering if the man was ok. "What would you recommend on a sunny day like today?" the man asked.

"Well, this depends on your plans," she replied, realizing she was getting the chance to practice her English. "If you have nothing important, I'd suggest a nice cold Prosecco accompanied by a cold glass of ancient Roman water. It's magical, you know."

"Magical, you say. I need a little magic, so that sounds fine," the old man replied, still catching his breath. As the young woman walked away, he settled into his chair and watched a family walk closer. The father was using his camera phone to film two lovely little girls. They circled him, smiling and giggling as he turned his head to follow them. Their mother followed, and the sunshine lit up the scene. As they passed his table, the family smiled at the man. He nodded, and the family took a nearby table.

He thought about his mother and father, who were long gone. And their memories were only faint in his mind. He could see his mother's face but couldn't remember her name or the sound of her voice. Thinking he might be cursed, he realized his deepest desire was to remember all the details of those moments from his life. He focused on the chirping Sparrows. The energy of gratitude lingered in his mind, but he wasn't sure why. It would have to be the people he'd known and all those moments they'd spent together. It was the places he'd been and the things he'd done. And it was the creative work that he loved and cherished, but the details were sparse.

He thought about all the different chapters that had come and gone. They were just glints and flashes now, ideas that came and went, all mixed into what he saw when his eyes were open. He wondered if anyone would remember him when he was gone, which was sure to happen soon. Maybe a few friends would think about him occasionally and smile, but so many of them were already gone. And If he couldn't remember their names, they certainly wouldn't remember his. His throbbing headache made everything seem like a purgatory. Death was such a dark and final thing, but in the last few months, he began to understand it differently as a blessing. Like his mother and father and their mother and father, he would become just another name on a genealogy chart. The funny thing was, he couldn't remember his name either. He giggled to himself at the absurdity of it all.

The young woman returned and placed two glasses and a pitcher on the table. "Prosecco and Roman water. The water is magical, you know." The young woman looked around and then back at the man. "I wish I could sit and enjoy the sunshine with you," she said, standing over him patiently. "Grazie mille signora," he replied. "My pleasure," she beamed, standing still momentarily as they both looked across the cobblestone street at the fountain in the town's square. "You know the fountain is 265 years old", she said, still staring. The man shrugged. "It's a source of great magic. They have often repaired it, but most of the fountain's structure is original. It was hand-carved and took hundreds of people many years to complete. A million person-hours to create or something like that."

The woman saw the man sweating, breathing heavily. Without asking, she dipped a cloth napkin into the pitcher of ice water, then ran it over the man's forehead. "Isn't that better?" she asked. "Yes, thank you," he replied in a meek tone. He looked at the drinks on the table but was too weak to lift his hand. "Do you see the three roads leading into the square?" the woman asked with her hand pointing. The man nodded. "Um, hmm, yes."

"They called it the Trevi Fountain because of the three roads which lead here." The man stared at the beautiful thing, trying to stay present. "The fountain sits on the original site of Acqua Vergine, an ancient aqueduct serving clean water to Rome for thousands of years. It's the same water that fills your glass today." The man nodded. "And as the story goes, with the help of a virgin, several Roman technicians channeled the magic so they could locate the source of this pure water many miles from here. Then, they constructed an aqueduct to carry the water directly to that fountain for all to share. You can see the story illustrated on its facade just there", she pointed again.

He felt enough energy as she spoke to lift the water glass to his mouth. The tasty liquid cooled his dry mouth and throat. From his gut, the water seemed to wake up his arms, hands, legs, and feet. He felt relieved. Perhaps this was magic water, he thought. The man looked up at the woman and was happy because, at that moment, his pain began to subside. "Could you tell me more about the fountain?" he asked. The woman surveyed the cafe's customers, and seeing they were content, she sat down at the table with the old man. She stared at the fountain for a moment, then spoke.

"The central figure in front of the large dome niche is Neptune, God of the sea. He's riding a triumphal chariot in the shape of a seashell. Pulling him across his domain are two Tritons. One horse is calm, and the other is restless. One Triton is strong and young; the other is older. The older Triton is holding a large twisted shell it uses to announce and clear room for their passage."

The man watched the young woman's eyes sparkle in the sun while she spoke. She wasn't looking at him but instead at the fountain. He used the opportunity to study the details of her face. He recognized her wisdom and kindness, which satisfied him. This world he'd be leaving would be left in good hands. She spoke softly, but her powerful words filled his imagination, luring his attention away from all the dark notions that consumed him. He was becoming more relaxed, realizing the pain was most certainly evaporating. He could feel it losing grip on his bones. He felt his muscles relax, and the old man began to feel centered.

Another couple walked up and sat down at an empty table. They smiled at the man and then picked up their menus. "I'll be right back," the young woman said, then greeted her new customers. The sun beat down and warmed his face, and the man realized he was beginning to feel relatively good for the first time in a long while. Nearly two years of discomfort had become his life, but suddenly, he felt hopeful again. He remembered that life had peaks, not just valleys. His mind felt clearer, but still, there was so much missing. He wondered what brought on this delightful surge and respite from the pain. Was it the Roman water or the Prosecco? Was it the young woman or her story about the fountain? Was it the sun, or was this just a dream from which he would soon awake to another day filled with pain? He thought about the two horses pulling Neptune, one calm and one restless. He likened them to the cells in his body, some calm, some restless. The women came back and sat down again.

"Signore, I must tell you, I find your story of the fountain fascinating, and I'm enjoying this moment. Would you tell me more?" he asked. "I will tell you everything I know," the woman answered with a clever smile, then began pointing and speaking. "The first statue on the left holds the horn of plenty, symbolizing the abundance of fruits. The second holds ears of wheat, which represent the fertility of crops. The third is holding a cup with bunches of grapes, symbolizing the earth's products of autumn. The last statue, which is female, depicts the joy of prairies and gardens and is adorned with flowers. You'll see a toppled vase used to gather water at her feet. Above her, you'll see a relief depicting Agrippa. "Agrippa," the old man repeated.

"Si, Agrippa was responsible for constructing Rome. He was a statesman, a general, and an architect. You can see Agrippa commanding his generals to build the Roman aqueduct. On the right side of the fountain is the Statue of Health, crowned by a wreath of laurel. He is holding a cup from which a snake drinks."

"A snake drinks from his cup?" the man said in

astonishment. "Is the snake good or bad? Does it bring health or disease?" The woman thought about the question. "I guess it depends on how you feel about snakes," the woman replied through laughter. "Many things, external and internal, cause disease. One man's poison is another man's cure. The symbol of medicine is called a Caduceus. It's a snake coiling itself to hold on tight." The man stared at the fountain in awe. "Yes, I remember that symbol," the man replied as he took another gulp of the Roman water.

"Perhaps knowing what to hold on to and what to let go of is the hardest thing to learn," the woman replied, taking her eyes off the fountain and staring at the man. The man thought about the woman's words and the story of the fountain. He wished he could remember. He wished there was a cure for his disease. But he also knew that the natural way was that no man should live forever. He did feel better. Finding this cafe was a miracle, something close to God's blessing.

The water in the fountain twinkled in the sun. And then his memories began returning like a river set free. First, his name, Stefano, and the memory of his youth returned all at once. He could hear his mother's voice again and imagine her face as she beamed with so much love. He recalled his father and sisters. He listened to the young woman speak and began to remember his wife and the decades of happiness they shared. As his precious memories flooded back, he felt hope again and excitement, too, and he wasn't sure why. The young woman could see the man had finally perked up. "Why don't you run your hands in the fountain water?" she suggested. "Legend has it that the water turns old men young."

"You know so much about the fountain," the man said.

"Yes, well, I grew up just two streets over," she admitted. "My father worked for the city, maintaining and protecting many of its treasures like the fountain." The man could only stare at the woman, so she gently pulled his chair out. The sun was turning orange now, and as he stood up, the man noticed the café was full, and all the patrons were smiling. He felt terrific as he walked towards the stunning fountain. He submerged one hand in the cool water and then the other, feeling a chill move up his spine. He splashed a little on his face.

In an instant, his entire life's memories and all the details returned in such a rush that he laughed and cried simultaneously. He looked up at Neptune, who was now familiar, and a tear rolled down his cheek and into the fountain's water. As the man returned to the cafe, he watched everyone rise from their chairs. To his surprise, the young woman was now holding a large cake filled with so many lit candles that it illuminated her face with a beautiful orange glow. And she moved towards him, beaming in her familiar way. He looked at the faces staring and knew each of their names. They were his family, friends, and everyone in his life. They gathered around him.

"Happy birthday, father," the young woman said. He felt a peace come over him that few men could ever know. He didn't need magic water and wasn't bargaining for more time. He had known happiness and good fortune. The man had been blessed with the riches of a lifetime's worth of experiences and was grateful for his incredible journey. He stared at all the faces around him and smiled. Then the man took a deep breath and blew out the candles on his last birthday cake.

Rules are rules

I just finished brushing my teeth, and I'm always pleased with how nice it feels to have a clean mouth. Bacterial buildup was a problem I failed to predict, but the toothbrush certainly solved that, didn't it? My hair is getting so long now; it's way past my shoulders. I enjoy combing my hair and letting the bristles massage the scalp; that really gets the blood going, doesn't it? Through the bathroom window, I can see my dad in the yard with his attention focused on the riding mower. I hear music playing and smell food cooking, so I head downstairs and pull up a chair at the dining room table. I enjoy the smell of coffee, but I don't like the taste. The side effect of having an immature pallet is a relatively narrow set of preferences and an acute resistance to sampling new food types. I never planned that; it was something nature did all by itself as a defense mechanism to protect newborns and children from ingesting foods that may be dangerous to their undeveloped digestive systems. Today is Saturday, and this is the five hundred and forty-seventh Saturday I've spent being Ida.

My mother filled her blue pitcher with orange juice and put it on the table. The pitcher is special to her. The outside is hand-painted, and the blue glazed finish is bright and eye-catching. It's a scene where a man works in a field using a long saw blade. The man saws stalks of straw or stalks of something and he's putting the cuttings into a basket. My mother noticed the pitcher a few months ago, and since it matched our blue plates, she bought it. It was the heaviest pitcher I ever picked up, too. It has a small, awkward handle, which makes it hard to pour. Since mom liked it so much, I always worried I might drop it, maybe even break it. I was extra careful when I picked it up and filled my glass. But even though I was scared of ruining it, it occurred to me that I could fix it with my power as long as I didn't make too large a ripple. You see, I'm not just a ten-year-old girl; I am God, creator of the universe. Since I try hard to live in the moment and enjoy being ten, I purposely forget that I can do anything. And ignoring all the God stuff is precisely what I'm trying to achieve. The radio was on, and I knew the song.

I would climb any mountain, sail across a stormy sea. If that's what it takes me, baby, to show how much you mean to me. And I guess it's just the woman in you that brings out the man in me. I know I can't help myself. You're all in the world to me...

I know the words to lots of songs. We are always listening to the radio, especially my brother Kevin. Kevin joined the army, and we haven't seen him in a long time. Kevin is a great brother. He once pulled me out of the water ditch when I slipped and fell in. After saving me, I watched him cry. He was so scared that I might have hurt myself or died. He really loves me, and I love him. It's fantastic to know and care for someone, whether they're your family or a friend, isn't it?

My mother put a nice-looking pile of eggs and bacon on my plate. The eggs were scrambled but folded repeatedly, forming these little ridges, which I like. My mom is a good mother. She always says, "Ida May Bloom," do you know how much I love you?" Then, she pulls my hands apart to show me how much she adores me. She stretches my arms as far as she can. That always makes me laugh. She really loves me; she really does. Ida May Bloom sounds like a country name, but it's not. Our family is very proud of our Bloom name. We even have a plaque in the living room that reads, *Bloom where you are planted*, and our mailbox reads, *The Bloom family*.

We aren't farmers; we're just an average family living in a rural neighborhood in West Texas. I'm ordinary, too, just a normal, average 10-year-old girl. But I want to be clear so you understand. Every so often, I live out the life of a human from the beginning to the end. I'm God, but I can enjoy the simplicity of just being Ida. I appreciate seeing the world I created through Ida's eyes. I relish feeling what Ida sees, hears, and senses; what she learns and experiences in herself. I enjoy the limitations and innocence of Ida's perceptions and her developing consciousness because it creates a unique point of view that I could never have experienced without being right here. And it always feels like the first time.

After breakfast, I kissed Mom and jumped out the

front door. I smell the hot sun and trees and hear cicadas screeching. Dad was in the front and asked me to move my bike and skates to the backyard, so I did. He asked how I planned to spend my day. Dad was always asking questions like that. He always asked all sorts of questions, and then he'd just smile and wait for me to answer. He does an excellent job of making me think more about all kinds of things. When you take a moment to think about something and really use your brain, there is a lot more to it, isn't there? I told him I would spend the day taking a closer look at the people and things around me. I said I wanted to learn the art of observation. I knew he'd like that because it's what he'd always tell me. Boy, that felt good to say, and he really seemed to like the idea. My father looked up at the morning sky; when he did, I did, too. We watched the clouds rolling by. My dad calls himself semi-retired and mostly reads books and magazines or works around the house. He also plays golf with friends and our neighbors. It's pretty simple around here.

The whole valley where we live is mostly cotton fields. We have a cotton field in the back of our house, but it's not ours. Some of the land is ours, but most isn't. We don't tend to the field; we aren't farmers or anything like that. A large irrigation ditch runs right next to our house and feeds water to all the cotton fields around here. It runs 2 miles towards the valley and 2 miles towards the mountains. We call it the ditch. The Rio-Grande River is close, but the ditch isn't connected.

The ditch is almost overflowing with water today, and the current is really going. There's grass and dirt on top of the water; you can see how powerful the water is by how fast the grass floats. There are crayfish in there, too. Sometimes, the water is shallow, and you can catch one. All the kids try to catch them, but no one ever can. Catching crayfish is easy if you have the right tool, and I do. I taped a small picnic basket to the end of a mop handle. The crayfish rest on the side of the ditch wall when the water is low. You need to be quiet, then slowly move the basket underneath to scoop them up. Some people call them crawdads, but I call them crayfish. We don't eat them; I just look at them and throw them back. Boy, was the water flowing fast today.

Now, if I make a right and follow the ditch in that direction, I end up at school. That's Zach White Elementary. I think Zach White was a sort of hero to folks around here. There's a picture of him in front of the school lobby, along with other people who lived long ago. If I make a left and walk down the ditch in that direction, there are more houses and then a place we call the gulley. If you wander past the gulley, there's an outdoor flea market, some more homes, and a pecan orchard way past that. I don't know what's past the pecan orchard, but I may get that far today. So I turned left, a choice Ida would think about for the rest of her life.

Heather Porter's house was just two from ours but on the other side of the ditch. Walking down the ditch and crossing the culvert, I saw Heather in her backyard. Heather's my best friend. She loves me, and I know that because I'm in that small group she thinks about. I adore Heather, too; we've been friends since kindergarten. Heather has a brother named Graham, and last year, he stole my bag of marbles. He took them from our house, but Heather didn't know. When Ida noticed her marbles were missing, I got mad. And I'll admit it: I cheated and used my god power just a little and knew that Graham had taken them.

I'll admit that I intervened for the first time in Ida's life. I felt so angry that someone had taken my marbles that I crossed the line, but just a little. I put the thought of him stealing my marbles in Graham's father's head. When I think about something, then it happens. Then, when his father found my marbles in Graham's dresser drawer, the rest came automatically. I only set the wheels in motion. I wanted those marbles back, you know? Heather's father made Graham return them and apologize. I wasn't mad; it didn't matter anyway because his sister Heather was my best friend.

So I approached Heather's house and saw her sitting at a picnic table in the backyard. She played with a large pink panther doll her father bought at the airport. The panther doll had an F.M. radio in its chest, and there were two knobs, one for volume and one for tuning the station. I could hear music and see she was moving her head to the beat of the music. She was a cool girl. Heather's hair looked perfect, falling on her forehead like a commercial.

Heather saw me, so she went to the fence, put her arms over it, and hugged like we always did. After I hugged her, Heather asked me if I was going to the flea market. "Cool idea," I told her and asked if she wanted to come. Then Heather ran inside the house and was gone for a minute. She ran back outside holding a big old carving knife. The girl looked like a maniac and came to the picnic table with a strange look. She raised the knife up and then began stabbing the pink panther in the chest. Seeing her carve open the doll's chest scared me a little. Watching all that pink hair blowing around her in a mini tornado was excellent, but I added the swirling wind for dramatic effect using my God power. She cut and tore at the doll's chest. Then, she managed to pull out the little gray radio. She threw the mutilated puppet carcass on the patio along with the carving knife. The radio had hunks of pink hair still attached, so she twisted the hair into bundles around her finger and pulled them off. Once the little radio was clean, she turned the knob, and it still worked. She jumped over their wooden fence, and we started walking up the ditch road, listening to that little gray radio.

While we walked, Heather would pick flowers from alongside the ditch and pop the flower's head from the stem with her thumb. "Momma had a baby, and its head popped off." She'd aim all the flower heads into the ditch. She was always mutilating puppets and flowers; she really was. After she'd pop the flower head in the water, it would float down in the opposite direction we were walking, you know, back towards my house. After we strolled a little more, I stopped and looked back. It was strange; the current caused the flowers to line up in a row right down the middle of the stream. The first flower head was nearly past my house already. I stopped walking again to watch them disappear. It really looks familiar, doesn't it? You could see all the way down the ditch, but the reflection was too bright to see clearly at the end. The water reflected the sun and made shiny silver and orange dots, which was beautiful. A cool breeze blew around us, and it felt so lovely. The cicadas were really screeching. Isn't this great? I thought.

We were initially quiet while we walked, feeling the sun and wind and listening to that little gray radio. Usually, we'd be talking about what our weddings would be like, who would be there, and what we'd be wearing. Sometimes we would talk about our husband's jobs, their names, or how we would force our children to play together. Heather and I would be best friends for our entire lives and were excited about that. Heather told me she French kissed David Dasso. David was a year older. David is going in the sixth grade. Heather and I were going into the fifth, but I knew exactly who she was talking about. My dad played golf with David's dad. He was a cute kid and really lovely, too. He visited our house for a New Year's party last year. I remember especially because it turned 1980, and everyone wore hats that read, *Kiss Me, It's Midnight!* The numbers on the hat were silver, and everyone was so excited. David didn't stay till midnight, but he was there, so I knew who she was talking about.

I kissed a boy named Roger Callahan two different times. The first time, we were on the playground after school on the merry-go-round. He was pushing us so fast, and no one else was around. We were spinning round and round, and he just did it; he kissed me. He really did, and I let him do it, too. It was just a kiss, but it was magic, really. It wasn't just physical; it was mostly in my head. I never planned any of that when I wished for the universe; nature's systems did a lot of that by itself over a long period, and the interactions were practically destined to make things happen the way they do. Physics, life, consciousness. It's incredible to see and feel how this whole system works from the inside.

Anyway, after Roger kissed me, he'd always smile at me and try to sit with me in the cafeteria. He'd buy me a snow cone after school. His mom would give him a dollar, and lunch was 45 cents, so he always had 55 cents left, enough for 2 cones cause they were a quarter each. I always chose the blue flavor, which was coconut. The second time he kissed me, we walked home from school and played on a culvert. The ditch has culverts near everyone's house, like a small metal bridge with a wheel in the middle. If you turn the wheel, you can open a small door at the side of the ditch and let water through. A metal tube under the ground at each culvert can open to allow water in any field. My father allowed me to open the tube in our yard once.

So we were on the culvert, and can you believe it,

Roger kissed me again. He just moved his head in and kissed me, and I let him do it again. I was just beginning to like him, but then he let the water run out into someone's yard we didn't even know. We didn't even know them, and he opened that culvert for no reason and let a thousand gallons of water into their yard. He flooded the whole back of that house, too. Watching all that water pour in so fast was scary, and I felt terrible about it. I didn't let Roger kiss me again after that.

So Heather and I are walking and talking about French kissing. Suddenly, the song Xanadu came on, and Heather looked at me. We started smiling because we knew the way the music sparkled. You just knew it right away. We both started singing to the music.

A place where nobody dared to go...the love that we came to know...they call it Xanadu...And now, open your eyes and see what we have made is real. We are in Xanadu.

The sunshine was warm on my face, and the music was so clear that it stayed in my head and chest while we sang. I got lost in the moment and didn't have to think about the universe and all those things that needed tending to. And I knew I was happy and that I was alive. I could feel the moment happening just as Ida did. And I had a friend, a best friend. And Heather would be my best friend, Ida's best friend for her, my entire life. Surely, this feeling couldn't' be duplicated. I can separate being a girl and being God to see how unforgettable these tiny moments are. I can step back and see how wonderful this girl feels, and I could feel it as her, as Ida, even knowing that I was, that I am God. I can do all of that. After all, I am God. I only have a few rules.

After the song, we passed Mr. Wiley's house, the last house on the right. His house looked more like a barn than a house. It was dark brown, and the paint was peeling and cracking off. It must be 100 years old. Sometimes, he'd give us apples or pecans, but he wasn't there today. After Mr. Wiley's house, the ditch runs through a dried-up field where no one lives; we call it the gulley. The gulley has a large hill on one side and an old junkyard on the other. The junkyard must be 30 years old, and there's all sorts of stuff to see there; old cars, refrigerators, swamp coolers, tons of old farm equipment, wheels, and even old boats. Close to the center of the junkyard is an old school bus. You can even pry open the door and sit in the bus if you want to. We used to play marbles in there. It's easy to shoot marbles in there because the aisle has small grates that run all the way down. But it gets hot in there, and it smells pretty gross.

There was a nice-looking C.B. radio in that old bus, and we used to play with it. It still worked and everything, and we'd talk to truckers. "Breaker one nine for radio check, you got yer ears on, come back." Anyway, the last time I was inside that old bus, I saw the C.B. was gone. Someone had ripped it right out of the dashboard. I got angry thinking someone would just take it like that. What about all the kids that played with it? I wanted to use my God power to punish whoever did it, but I couldn't experience things like Ida and use those powers all the time. At this very moment, I'm focused on trillions of thoughts. It's mainly watching but sometimes stepping in to make adjustments. I can separate those things from the here and now, though. I create a wall so I can enjoy being a 10-year-old girl. Anyway, people are always stealing stuff, you know.

Heather threw a large rock at a pile of glass windows stacked against an old El Camino. We both started hurling rocks and smashing what was left of those glass sheets. I threw a rock at an air conditioner and smashed the taillight on that old car. Heather carved her name into the hood after breaking off the car's radio antenna. Then she scribbled it out, saying she didn't want anyone to know it was her. She's always getting nervous about that kind of stuff. I spotted an old field tractor and began hurling rocks at it. I picked up the air conditioner and lobbed it at the tractor pretty hard when I was out of rocks. When it hit, the tractor split into two and sent shards of metal debris into the sky. A nifty little mushroom cloud of dust and smoke rose, too, but I didn't let Heather see that. No harm was done, and I didn't break the rules.

It was a hot day, and Heather and I were a little sweaty now. We continued past the junkyard to the other end of the gulley and could see across the street. There were a lot of people at the flea market. We went to the street's edge and ran across when the traffic was clear. There was a ton of stuff for sale in the parking lot. There were Mexican blankets, pots, and paintings. There were rings, bracelets, and a whole vegetable stand with corn, onions, apples, pecans, and watermelons. One guy sold plastic animals; another stand had statues he made from spare metal pieces welded together to form odd-looking creatures. I don't usually buy stuff there, but it's fun just to people-watch. There are always a bunch of vans lined up with their back doors open so you can see all the other stuff they have to sell.

At the end of the lot, there's a store called Logan's; we always go in there. They have those long, icy popsicles and only one arcade game. Now get ready because it's freezing when you walk in. They always had the air conditioner on full blast. Before we walked in, Heather pulled a ten-dollar bill from her pocket. She quickly flicked the ends apart to make that paper-smacking noise. "Cash is king," she said. I never knew what that meant, but we both smiled. She got quarters from the cashier, and we understood what was coming. And we walked towards it feeling so excited. It's a video game we like to play called Space Zap. It's about the oldest video game in the world, but it's still fun to play. There are only four buttons: right, left, top, and bottom. When an alien comes at you, you fire that button to blow up their ship. At first, the aliens come slow, then they come quicker and faster, and you better hit the buttons quicker and faster, too. It makes me feel nervous when it gets too fast. Heather put in a quarter; I just watched. The first aliens were easy, but the quicker it got, the more Heather would let out little noises like she was in pain, like someone was burning her with matches or a hot poker. It made me chuckle because she squeaks and gets even more nervous than I do. Her tongue comes out and makes a point, too. It's embarrassing, really. She was totally out of control.

You can't win Space Zap; they just want you to keep putting quarters in. Heather always gets at least one of the high scores and leaves her initials so everyone will know it. Number 4 on the list with 28,250 points is H.M.P. That stands for Heather Marie Porter. Heather bought us two red popsicles when we finished, and we headed out. The minute you got back outside, you could feel it; the heat and sun were right on you again. It always feels great to step out into the heat and sunshine; boy, did they keep that place cold.

We headed to a small jewelry stand in the flea market parking lot. A woman came out of the back of a van and walked up behind the jewelry display. She had a feather in her hair. Heather tried on bracelets and a few rings, then settled for a silver ring with a turquoise stone in the center. She asked the woman how much, and the woman said five dollars. Now, I wasn't using my God power or anything, but I got the strange feeling she said three dollars to someone else just a few minutes before when we were playing Space Zap. Ok, I knew it because I used my God power. Boy, Ida has used the God power a lot lately, but it's just tiny stuff; no rules have been broken.

But the truth is that the smiling woman with a feather in her hair is now trying to cheat my best friend. Heather doesn't know it either. I decided to use my God power and give the women a suggestion. It's like pushing a toy car in the direction you want it to go. I know it was cheating and that I wouldn't be able to do that if I were a regular human girl, but I loved Heather, and that clouded my judgment. You knew humans had free will, right? Well, I am human, after all. The woman said she had made a mistake: the ring was 3 dollars. Heather gave her a five and got 2 dollars change. The women smiled, and so did Heather. I grinned, too. What a great day we were having.

When I created the universe and this relatively tiny world, I set it into motion so that it could operate independently. Everything that happens is a direct result of something that occurred previously. The whole thing was set into motion a long time ago, very much like the toppling of a single domino. I'm telling you this because here's where the story may get a little sad for you, and I'm sorry for that.

With popsicles in hand, we headed back to the other end of the flea market parking lot. Heather was turning her wrist back and forth to make the ring sparkle in the sun. She was hypnotized, and I loved seeing her so happy, but we had to cross the street again. I ran ahead of her without really noticing she was lagging behind. I shouldn't have because I knew she was preoccupied with that new ring. When I reached the other side, I turned to look back and saw Heather step off the curb, still admiring the ring. She didn't notice the tan car trying to make the yellow light. I saw her look up and realize the mistake. I watched the car hit her. The impact was hard; the horn honked, and the tires screeched. I watched Heather hit the windshield, and then she rolled off onto the street. This was really happening, and I had a hard time understanding it. I have felt many things as God and Ida, but this was so unfamiliar that I couldn't fully appreciate what was happening. It was like I was trapped just staring, and that was strange. Of course, the people at the flea market ran over to Heather, and I did, too.

I was holding her hand, and she looked at me. I watched the sun and blue sky reflect in her eyes. She didn't say anything. And then she was just gone. Heather died. The impact had broken her neck and shattered her spine. I knew exactly what happened to her; I could see it without breaking any rules. I noticed the people around us begin to cry. Then Ida realized what had happened to Heather and started crying, too. I was crying. The crying gave way to hysteria, anger, and fear. I remember thinking this would be too much to use my God power. The ripple would go too far. I could never make an exception for something as trivial as this. You must understand that this was trivial in the larger scheme of things, and rules are rules. I had to separate the emotions and feelings of a child and the small handful of people affected by this.

Heather's death was no different than a planet forming, a star burning out, or a river carving a path through a mountain. It was the result of multiple previous events, and too many people were involved now. Bringing her back would be very different than putting a thought in one person's head or learning about someone stealing a bag of marbles. I'd have to back time up, and the ripple would be too large. I looked ahead and saw that a crosswalk and a new traffic light system would be installed at this intersection, and that's good, isn't it? Heather's death would prevent others if you followed causality out far enough. I went over it again and again, but rules are rules. I can't make an exception just because I'm personally involved. Ida would get over it soon enough; after all, death is a natural part of life. People die. It was observed by many others - it had become real. What could I do? That was a day I always thought about, both as Ida and God.

Ida is forty-two years old now and has two children and a husband. I have P.T.A., choir, bake sales, and soccer practice. My husband and I spend time with our children, family, and friends. I am a teacher at Zach White Elementary, and my children go there, too. And I spend plenty of time with my best friend, Heather Porter. Well, it's Heather Dasso now. No, no, Heather is not dead. Heather ended up marrying David, and they have two beautiful children. She's still my best friend, and as a matter of fact, we still live in the same neighborhood.

We often talk about that warm, sunny Saturday and all the Saturdays that came after. That Saturday is one of our fondest memories from childhood. And every time we talk about it, we thank God she wasn't hurt by that speeding car. That always makes me smile. Look, I had a change of heart, ok? I made a few adjustments, and the ripple was within limits. I added a pinch of reaction time over here, a little more breaking distance over there, and presto, just a close call and a good story. We spent the rest of that Saturday giggling, laughing, and singing with that little gray radio. It was a perfect day.

That's also the afternoon I decided that any rule can be broken, no matter how big and for any reason I chose. You see, I learned that a rule is only a rule when someone with more power than you can enforce it. And I realized something - No one can tell me what to do; I am God.

Cassidy Got Lucky

Ya'll, cmon aboard for a tale about a fella from West Texas named Cassidy Clementine. He's generally a good kid, kept his saddle oiled and his gun greased but he'd surrounded hisself with banditos, scuz buckets and all sorts a criminal types. The whole lot wuz a bad influence on the boy. And since his momma went and died and his daddy had up and left em when he wuz knee-high to a grasshopper, the boy got no real discipline. As one might expect, by age 21, Cassidy wuz gittin in all sortsa trouble with the law for lowlife thievin and such. This wuz the tippin point in his young life. It wuz either clean up and folla the law or get used to a life of bein in-an-outta jail. As one might imagine, the kid wuz bowed up from bein poor white trash and not havin a daddy and all. Any mule's tail can catch burrs but pickin em off is the hard part. Besides that, all the other fellas Cassidy knew wuz paintin they tonsils with the devil's elixir every dam night. Yes sir, all his amigos wuz-a-puffin on that Mexican tobaccy, stayin out all night snortin up that dam Columbian powder and takin part in all sorts of deviltry.

Now listen here; in the apartment, just 1 over from Cassidy wuz this old Indian woman. She sorta took a likin to the boy, wuz good to em, always lookin out fer em and whatnot. She knew Cassidy's amigos wuz nuthin but trouble and about as helpful as an outhouse breeze. She wuz real patient with the boy keepin an eye and tryin to teach him to do right. But that ole Indian woman had an uphill battle. You see, Cassidy didn't know any better on accounta all them bad influences round these here parts. He wuz impressionable, just imitatin what other fellers had done. Cassidy knew more ways to steal yer money than a roomful a lawyers. Hell, he wuz bustin' into houses by age 14. That boy'd spot a fine-lookin house, slide in some busted winda, and get to lootin.

Just recently, Cassidy took the Mexican motto, mi casa es su casa, a lil too far and won hisself a free pair a silver bracelets. The judge sentenced Cassidy to 30 days in the pokey on accounta hes just a misguided youth and all. Cassidy had just been released, and the rent on his apartment wuz past due. He figured he'd find his duds and whatnot out by the dumpster but you know what? That ole Indian woman paid Cassidys rent. She told the boy he could get square once he's back on his feet n-all. The other problem wuz the dang judge put em on probation an ordered him to pay $2500 in fines. Speakin in plain terms, that wuz a hellova lot of loot for a 21-year-old. An to make matters worse, the judge ordered Cassidy to work 300 community hours for the good-a-tha community and all. In addition, the kid wuz gonna hafta report to his probation officer every month to get piss tested and whatnot. Now this wuz the time for Cassidy to set aside all the lawlessness and conform to all them rules of polite society which for all intensive purposes meant ta get a dang job.

Over all else, the boy's dream wuz movin to the Florida Keys so he could live by the ocean and do as he pleased. But the beaches and Florida wuz gonna hafta wait till he got off probation. His second-best dream wuz to be one of them fancy waiters over at Billy's joint. Billys wuz a real fancy tenderloin right on the border of Texas an New Mexico. It had been rumored them boys over at Billys wuz makin 3, 4, sometimes 5 hundred a night. One feller had made hisself a $1200 dollar tip when a couple-a dealers left him 2 grand on a 800 dollar bill. Bein a waiter at Billy's meant you had to wear a button up shirt and bowtie, but it wuz worth gettin gussied up for all the scratch they wuz haulin. Cassidy had applied several times but wuz told they simply wuzn't hirin no one. Oh he kept on lookin, eyeballin the papers, fillin out employment questionnaires at various establishments and whatnot.

Naggin got to be a thing for that ole Indian woman. She got to hootin and hollerin bout his rent comin and putin grub in his own icebox. Hell, Cassidy wuz so poor If a trip around the world cost a dollar, the boy couldn't get to the Oklahoma state line. Lookin fer-a job and gettin chewed out by his neighbor came to be routine an the kid felt he wuz barkin at a knot. Just then, whilst feelin sorry for hisself, he spotted a real daisy in the paper. It said Pawn Shop Representative. Yes, sir, it wuz a job! Now ifin you dont know, Texas is real big. Ole Wallace used to say, in the covered wagon days, if a baby wuz born in Texarkana whilst the family wuz crossin the Lone Star State, by the time they reached El Paso, that dang babied be in the third grade.

Now since Cassidy didn't have a wagon, distance wuz a mucho problemo. But as circumstance had it, that there Pawn Shop job wuzn't nearly in Texarkana. In fact, it wuzn't but just a mile down the dam road from Cassidy's crumblin apartment complex. And you know what? Ya'll aint gonna believe the name neither. It wuz called Lucky's Pawn. Thank the lord that that ole Indian woman had a paid-up telephone line. Cassidy dialed the number and wuz told to come on in right then and there.

Now go figure, Lucky's Pawn Shop wuz owned by a big bug named Lucky Davis. Lucky wuz a real shit-kickin, tobacco-spittin, whiskey-drinkin Texan. He wore one a them Cattleman straw cowboy hats with the silver conchos. He had the big ass silver and turquoise belt buckle and one of them open-carry six-shooters, the whole nine. Yes sir, Lucky wuz a real redneck, didn't talk proper and mostly just cussed all the dam time. The interview wuz easy breezy on accounta Cassidy didn't sound much like a degenerate. I rekon he fibbed when he skipped over the part on the questionnaire bout had he ever been in trouble with the law and such. But Cassidy felt that bizness should be nothin to no one.

Wouldn't you know it, they hired our boy on the spot. I'm talkin winner, winner, chicken dinner. No reference check, no background check, not even a dang piss test. Nosir! You see, Cassidy had the outward appearance of respectability, and Lucky felt he could spot an honest soul. I sapose we all overestimate our abilities to some degree now and again.

Now, before we keep goin y'all should know Cassidy never thought a hisself as a criminal type. Like I said this wuz a tippin point in his young life. He wuz just a dumb kid who didn't grasp the notion of truth or consequences. But like I said, this wuz it: either go straight or live like an outlaw. He wuz smart enough and had a hell-of-a lot of pride for bein just another poor bastard livin in squalor. Cassidy imagined that if he could stay outta trouble and resist all them bad influences he'd come out ok. Hell, it wuz so many criminal types round these parts you could rake in any direction and graze a baker's dozen.

Anyhow, whilst they wuz trainin Cassidy to be a real expert in pawn shoppin at Luckys, he had hisself a gander round that shop. He put eyes on all the whatnots fillin the shelves and cases. He caught eyes with a butt ugly gal too. She wuz nuthin but white trash, had tattoos coverin her arms and neck. Turns out that ole gal wuz the dam shift manager. I rekon

Lucky wuz sweet on that filly-n gave that gal the job. There wuz another employee, an ugly Mexican fella. His face looked like six miles of busted asphalt, and he hardly had any dam teeth. That fella wuz runnin the army surplus section for Lucky. Look folks, here's the deal, this establishment wuz a genuine shit hole. And these people wuz takin terrible advantage of poor folks in their most desperate hour. Cassidy knew right away this wuz no kinda place for him but he wuz so poor his Sunday supper wuz fried water. It goes without sayin he needed the job.

First few days wuz easy breezy. He stood around learnin the pawnin business. He only had to watch the customers as they came in haulin all sorts of odds and ends. Oh, they dragged in TVs and guitars, jewelry and rack stereos, 8-track players, CB radios, lawnmowers, tools, and construction equipment. But you know what else they had a slew of? GUNS! There wuz pistols and old Betsy's, lead shooters, Roscoe's, hand canons, persuaders and equalizers too. Now, it's a fact that God created man, but ole Sam Colt made em equal! And with all them dam guns piled up liecat, Luckys wuz spreadin equality for the good of all mankind. Cassidy put eyes on shotguns, deer rifles, buck knifes, brass knuckles, hell, it wuz even a whole shelf filled with switchblades and stilettos but not a goddam bible in sight.

Stay with me now. Real quick Cassidy learnt hisself the pawnin business. He saw all them poor mommas return to the shop on their payday to git back the family TV set, only to return with it just a few days later for another loan. He learned how to size up an item and come up with a price Lucky could sell it fer no matter. If they came back before the loan expired, Lucky made his interest, and ifin they didn't, Lucky could sell the merchandise clean.

Every pawn wuz recorded on a numbered ticket with 4 copys. There wuz the original and 3 carbons down below. The white copy wuz on top, and the customer got to keep her. Under it wuz a pink copy, which got filed in the cabinet behind the register. An the green copy went to a file in the back office for good measure. Now, the Yella copies got all bundled together an they wuz given to the police every month so they could check em against burglaries and stickups. The last step wuz puttin a sticker on whatever it wuz gettin pawned and to jot down the ticket number, so they could tell what wuz what.

Three weeks passed by. Now Cassidy wuz runnin his own pawns, collectin a paycheck, payin his rent and puttin grub in the icebox. He wuz in compliance with his PO, passin all his piss tests and settlin in a more responsible life. All the notions of livin a life a crime had been set aside. Toward the end of his second month at Luckys, Cassidy wuz told to bring in that pile a Yella pawn tickets to the police station. It wuz close too, just a 2-minute walk from the dang store. That white trash manager told Cassidy to get a receipt for his stack a tickets on accounta Lucky had to prove he wuz complyin with the law. Cassidy knew the joint too. He'd been in that dang jail least half a dozen times. I'm with Lucky's Pawn, he told the lawman through the glass. Then Cassidy just stared at that boy who wuz watchin Bonanza reruns behind that counter.

The dude hardly looked up but eventually led Cassidy down a hallway toward the back-a the station. They come to big ole storage room. Cassidy saw piles-n-piles a cardboard boxes filled with Yella pawn tickets. The lawman took the tickets from Cassidy and dropped that bundle in the box with Luckys Pawn written on the side in black magic marker. The cop nodded to Cassidy and turned to walk out, but Cassidy remembered. He said hey, I'm supposed to get a receipt for those tickets. That lawman bout pissed and moaned, but he wrote one up fer the kid anyhow. Cassidy stood there starin at them boxes a Yella pawn tickets. From the looks these wuz from all over the city. Years worth of sleaze bag pawn tickets just sittin in this unlocked and perty much unguarded room.

On the third visit to his PO, Cassidy wuz told they didn't like em workin at the pawn shop none on account of all the sleaze bags and scuz buckets peruzin about. Also, cuz all them dam guns and knives wuz stacked up likeat. Thankfully the dudes PO understood that jobs didn't grow on trees, especially round these parts. He wuz informed he had to start knockin out them community service hours or they wuz gonna revoke his probation and lock em up again. But luck wuz still on Cassidys side. That boys PO told him he could warsh police cars over at the station by his apartment - the same dam one just down the street from Luckys.

That next Saturday Cassidy Clementine wuz out front a that dam police station at 8 in the mornin with them other felons, drug addicts, burglars an degenerates. They got to warshin police cars, moppin hallways, scrubbin toilets, trimmin hedges, gatherin up tumbleweeds an paintin dumpsters. I guess if ya lie down with dogs you gonna get up with fleas. The lawman in charge of these fellers wuz called Roy, and he wuz a friendly type. I'd go so far as to say Roy felt sorry for them degenerates slavin away under the Texas sun whilst tryin to pay their debt to society. Sometimes Roy would double them hours fer fellas bustin hump. After a few weeks, Cassidy got friendly with Roy and figured he could knock out them 300 community hours in 2 er 3 months tops.

By good rights things shoulda been dandy but Cassidy wuz gettin bored. He wuz bored scrapin by, bored with not bendin his elbow with bug juice out at the bars an saloons he used to frequent. Bored of not socializin and meetin up with rafts of good-lookin buckle bunnies he could go off pirootin with. Heck, he wuzn't even allowed to head south of the border on accounta it wuz technicly leavin the country an that wuz sure to get him revoked. And as much as he loved that ole dam Indian woman, Cassidy wuz bored a gettin earfuls aher advice. He figured why shear a pig if he wuz gonna be a workin stiff. If he coulda just been patient, he'd knock out them hours, get in the good graces of his PO, and fly off to Florida and all them sunny beaches and palm trees. That's where the boy's dreams were waitin.

Around noon, Lucky and that white trash manager headed over to JJ's for some stank-ass menudo. Cassidy wuz wanderin that big ole store all by his lonesome and that Mexican fella wuz out back countin clouds. Cassidy got ta peekin at odds and ends. He figured no one wuz lyin awake thinkin bout all this here junk. He wandered to the jewelry case and that kid saw mucho dinero starin back. Some of them pieces wuz worth thousands. Half of them sparklers wuz pawned by women on account of their cheatin husbands. Yes, sir, they wuz hawkin engagement and wettin-rings then gettin the hell out of Dodge. The other half wuz hauled in by robbers and drug addicts cashin out late-night hauls. I suppose a few of em wuz pawned by freshly arrested drug dealers desperate to pay them lawyer retainers sows they could stay out the hoosegow. And let me tell you, a whole bunch of that jewelry appeared to be of the sort that only a dam drug dealer wuz wearin. Big thick ass gold nugget-lookin watches, bracelets and chains, thick rings and whatnot. Hell, wearin them things round these parts wuz runnin with the big dogs but it wuz probable cause in the eyes of the law. Cassidy reckoned there must have been a few hundred thousand dollars a gold in them dam cases.

Sure enough, Cassidy had allowed the reptilian portion of his cabeza to fill up with all sorts of misplaced notions, and the deviltry wuz once again sparklin in his eyes. Cassidy unlocked that dang case and pulled out a thick gold nugget watch. Goddam, it wuz heavy as hell. The little white sticker had the number 5742. He pulled it off and jammed that watch straight in his pocket, then he rearranged the watches in the case so there werent no empty space. He found that matchin pink ticket and took a gander. It wuz hocked bout a year back. Cassidy figured the feller wuz long gone or in the pokey. The loan had expired so it coulda been sold anyhow.

Cassidy tore up the pink copy and flushed it down the commode so no-one-wood be the wiser. He wuz just standin there thinkin on who he could call to pawn the watch for em when lightnin stuck. He'd almost overlooked the dam green copy. He walked his sorry ass to the back-office file, found that green copy, tore it up and sent it swirlin.

That night, when Cassidy got home, he used that ole Indian woman's telephone. He called a feller he knew called Jeff Mowery. Now, Jeff wuz a good ole boy and perfect for this line. He wuz hard up fer cash gamblin away all his scratch and had no morals whatsoever. They arranged for a 70/30 split in Cassidy's favor. Jeff wuz so dammed excited about the opportunity he jumped in his wagon and sped like the devil to meet up. Cmon now, people, stay wit me cuz this here is where the story starts gettin real good!

Well, good ole Jeff pulled into Cassidy's apartment complex like a rabid dog. The son-bitch wuz bright-eyed, honkin up a storm and likin' his chops to boot. Cassidy came out, pointed right at Jeff's face and shouted, listen here you degenerate gambler, you better do this right! He told Jeff that if he did good, they could keep it goin. Cassidy knew the law and it'd be tough for a lawman to connect him to Mowery even if his partner wuz wearin silver bracelets and got to yappin. Cassidy had flushed all the pawn tickets, so there ain't no record except for the Yeller copy at the police station, which bothered him some but he shook it off. Cassidy knew that sendin Jeff by his lonesome wuz about as sure as a lick and a promise. And Mowery wuz such a liar he'd beat you senseless and tell God you fell off a horse. Still, he wuzn't nearly about to risk his freedom hawkin a stolen watch, especially with a value over a grand. Son, thats a felony.

The next mornin, Cassidy heard a vehicle pull in the complex. Horror slid down the kid's back and his imagination jumped the track. The law must have Jeff in custody and that ignorant wobblin' jaw waddie had spilt his guts. Now the law wuz gonna haul Cassidy back to the hoosegow. My God what have I done he thought to hisself. His probation would be revoked, new charges filed, and Cassidy was gonna be lookin at hard time now - 2 or 3 years in the TDC, the Texas Deparment a Corrections. Aint no chance of gettin them felonies set aside or wipin his record clean now. His ship had sailed, and that ole Indian woman wuz gonna be crushed. The boy prayed for mercy directly to the good lord above. And you know what? God musta had his ears on cuz when Cassidy took a gander out the winda, he saw Jeff smilin and gigglin like a drunk fool. And that fella wuz holdin two fists fulla cash. Mowery had gotten $1,600 for that dam gold watch. Cassidy shook his head in relief whilst Jeff counted off his 70 percent, just over 11 hundred dollars. Hoowee Jackpot!

That mornin at Lucky's Pawn Shop nothin appeared out the ordinary. Mornin Cassidy, Lucky said from behind a newspaper. Morning Lucky, Cassidy said whilst he walked past the jewelry case shakin off regret. He glanced over to see whats what but nothin appeared outta place. That white trash manager wuz doin a once over on some Senoritas salon-style hair dryer. They both smiled at our boy as he passed em by. The mornin went on without a hitch. Lunch came and went. It wuz just bout closin time, an Cassidy had found hisself all by his lonesome once again. And that's the real testa character aint it? When aint no one lookin and ya can't escape yer own proclivities.

This time Cassidy spotted a real daisy, it wuz a thick ass gold nugget bracelet just wastin space. There had to be dozens a bracelets piled up. But this wuz the gaudiest, thickest dam gold bracelet he'd put eyes on. He figured it could be pawned for 2, maybe 3 grand. Sure enough, Cassidy had allowed the reptilian portion of his cabeza to lead em astray. He unlocked that case, snatched up that bracelet. He found the pink copy in the front cabinet. It wuz pawned for $2600 bout 6 months prior, and Cassidy thought he wuz dreamin when he put eyes on the ticket holder's name. It wuz a fella he knew called Freddie Kagan. They'd been in grade school together over at Mustang Elementary. He couldn't imagine how Freddie had come upon the bracelet in any legal sorta way. Maybe Freddie had done some burglerin of his own. The pawn wuz 5 months old, but the loan wuz fer 6 months. Cassidy wuz gonna have to wait 3 or 4 more weeks to be sure. But what wuz the odds that Freddie wuz comin back in the next few weeks? Cassidy took off the sticker, ripped up the pink and green tickets and sent em swirlin just like he'd done the last time.

He called Jeff again, and arranged another 70/30 split. Jeff came that night, took that dang bracelet then appeared again the next mornin. He'd got $2600 up in Las Cruces. Jeff counted $1,820 into Cassidy's palm. Nice work Amigo, Cassidy offered in a genuine sorta way. He paid that ole Indian woman back for the rent she loaned em but she'd gave em an earful when she seen all the cash. Now Cassidy wuz flush and wanted to let things cool off some.

Now listen here to whats comin cuz this part is real important. Just as Cassidy finished washin up his breakfast plate that ole Indian woman come over and said he had a telephone call. As luck would have it, the manager over at Billys Steak House wuz hirin! It seems one of their best fellas had got the helloutta Dodge an they had to replace em stright away. They wanted Cassidy and the shift manager at Billys promised they'd take real good care of em cuz he'd be quittin his job over at Luckys and all. Cassidy got to hootin and holerin and figured he wuz belly through the brush over them things he stole from Luckys. Besides he knew hisself and he'd be tempted to nibble if he stayed on. The kid phoned up that white trash manager at Lucky's and quit that dam job right then and there. And yes, Cassidy's PO and even that ole Indian woman wuz just thrilled about it all. Man wuz Cassidy burnin the breeze!

Let me tell you, in that bowtie Cassidy looked like one a them real fancy waiters. He wuz a natural at slangin steaks and fancy cocktails with them lil umbrellas. The folks here wuz mostly respectable, hardly any scum buckets er degenerates. Our dude wuz makin good scratch, and it wuz cash. And at quittin time there wuz a lounge out back at Billys where he could have hisself a few drinks and his PO would be none the wiser. Folks he knew from around town showed up. His first week wuz a hog-killin time.

The Theatre of Magic

Cassidy wuz makin good scratch, payin his court fines and rent and he wuz knockin out them community service hours with Roy over at the police station. He'd be startin his new life in the Florida Keys in no time. Another week past by and it wuz quittin time at Billys. Cassidy wuz flush with cash and headed to that lounge out back to paint his tonsils. He's gonna have hisself some wild mares' milk in every color of the rainbow. He wuz laughin and drinkin, tellin jokes and singin with his amigos when a feller he knew walked into that dang lounge. It was his old friend from Mustang Elementary, Freddie Kagen, the same feller whose bracelet he'd liberated from Luckys.

Now, Freedie was as welcome as a skunk at a lawn party. Cassidy turnt his eyes down and tried to look away, but as luck had it, Freddie and Cassidy got to starin. Naturally, they went to talkin and drinkin. They reminisced and whaled bout them good times from grade school. Wouldn't you know it, Freddie had a whole bunch of that dam Columbian powder, and the two took turns squarin off in the toilet. Them 2 hombres got high as a Mexican kite. Hell, ifn they got any higher theyd drop their harps plumb through the clouds. They wuz drinkin and snortin and got to hootin and holerin for hours.

Now, Cassidy wuz perty smart when he wuz sober but

when he got to drinkin, he caught a bad case-a loose lips. And when he wuz sniffin on that dam Columbian powder, hoowee did his jaw get to flappin. Cassidy got to jabbin bout how he'd quit at Luckys. And right then, Freddie started barkin back. Freedie confided that he got hisself $2,600 for pawnin his daddy's gold bracelet over at Luckys. It seems Freddie needed money to help his poor momma out a pickle. Worse yet, Freddie's daddy had given em the bracelet just before he'd gone up to heaven. Hearin Freddie's story, bout his daddy and all tugged at Cassidys heart. His mind wuz turnin in circles about that dam bracelet. Doin wrong il wreck a fella.

It had to be that dang Columbian powder cuz right then and there Cassidy confessed to nabbin Freddie's bracelet out the display case over at Luckys. Cassidy spilt the beans and told Freddie he wuz real sorry bout the whole dam mess. Cassidy felt so terrible inside that he told Freedie bout an ole pawn secret strictly enforced by Texas law. He told Freedie that if he wuz to go to Lucky's and present that original pawn ticket, they wuz gonna have to give him somethin for his trouble cuz Luckys wouldn't be able to come up with his daddys bracelet. And Cassidy told Freddie they wuznt gonna be able to find them pawn tickets neither cuz he'd flushed em. They wuz gonna have to compensate Freddie and there wuz nothin more to be said about it. Cassidy made Freddie swear to Jesus he'd keep his jaws clapped. But that wuz just a load, cuz aint no one can trust 2 toad swindlers eyein a prize.

A course, bright and early the next mornin, still percolatin, Freddie Kagen walked into Lucky's Pawn with that gold bracelets original white ticket in hand. He told em he wuz gonna repay the loan and get back his daddy's gold bracelet. As you can imagine, that white trash manager looked in the glass case, but nothin matched the ticket number. She looked fer the pink copy in the front file but couldn't find nothin. She looked fer the green copy too but we dam sure know she wuzn't gonna find hide nor hare. Her and Lucky searched the whole dam store fer the bracelet described on Freddie's pawn ticket, but we already know there aint nothin to find. No tickets, no bracelet.

Freddie started gettin impatient, told em it wuzn't right they'd lost his bracelet before the loan had expired and he demanded compensation. Freddie asked for $1200, the difference between what the bracelet wuz worth and what he'd already borrowed. Now, you gotta understand, Lucky wuz no saphead. Oh sure he wuz a redneck but the dude had good sense and got to eyeballin Freddie up and down.

Just then Lucky asked Freddie to show him the cash

he's gonna use to pay back the loan. As you can imagine, that went over like a lead balloon cuz Freddie didn't have but 3 dollars in his pocket. Things got heated and Freddie got flustered. The boy's head wuzn't right. Freedie had always been a few pickles short of a Barrel, especially that mornin. He told Lucky that if he couldn't come up with his bracelet or find them 2 other pawn tickets, that by Texas law, he'd have to be compensated. Once Lucky heard Freddie's words, he cocked his noggin to one side and got about as friendly as a fire ant. We aint never said nuthin bout losin pawn tickets son, where in tarnation did you get that notion? Freddie froze up, started starin at the floor an wonderin how it wuz that he might end up on the wrong side of the law. Lucky walked to the front door and locked it up tight. He turned that hangin sign from open to closed an told that white trash manager to call the police. Hell, you could hear Freddie gulp clear across the dam store.

Doc Holiday once said that conflict follows wrongdoin as surely as flies follow the herd. Sure enough, about two hours later, Cassidy saw a freshly washed police car pull up in his complex and a lawman started bangin on his door. He just knew it was Freedie. What in the hell had Freedie said? Cassidy opened with a friendly smile. The fella gave a shake and howdy as Detective so and so. Said there wuz a theft over at Lucky's Pawn, somethin bout a valuable bracelet had been nibbled by someone and he wuz fixin to find out who done it. And while that Detective wuz talkin, Cassidy could see them dam silver bracelets swingin in the breeze from the fellers back pocket. He knew the dude wuz there to arrest em ifn he didn't hear somethin to change his mind and quick! That boy's heart wuz poundin somethin fierce, but he pulled his boots up and kept it together.

The ole Indian woman was shakin her head but Cassidy invited the lawman to have a seat on his couch. As you might imagine Cassidy wuz thinkin bout gettin arrested, his probation gettin revoked, an goin back to the hoosegow. Yes sir, the kid wuz terrified an his guts wuz fillin up with regret. That lawman laid it on the line. Boy, listen here, we got a feller in custody called Freddie Kagen tellin us that you confessed to stealin a gold bracelet along with some pawn tickets when you wuz employed up at Lucky's.

Cassidy's mind wuz turnin like the whirlwind whilst the kid formulated the dangdest tale he could muster. Let me tell you something Detective so and so, Cassidy told the lawman. I've known Freddie Kagen since grade school and he's a thief, a liar and always sniffin on that dam columbian powder. I'll tell you exactly what happened. I wuz working at Billys last night and who walks in but Freddie Kagen. We wuz drinkin and talkin. Naturally, I told em I'd quit my job at Lucky's a couple weeks back. After a few whiskeys, Freddie went on bout how he knew the place and that he'd pawned a gold bracelet a while back. Freddie told me that after the woman handed him the pawn money, that she turned her back to help another customer, and that's when Freedie snatched up that bracelet and the pawn tickets from on top the counter. Then he walked right out the store with the whole dam lot. He seemed proud to have gotten away with it. Hell, it wuz like he wuz braggin. I admit I told Freddie that they'd have to give him some sort of compensation if he returned with that original ticket but that wuz just my whiskey talkin. If the dumb son bitch tried it, that aint on me. Now Cassidy wuz workin for his freedom and he put up a humdinger oscar performance. That ole lawman stared into Cassidy's eyes and dam near got hypnotized.

Detective so and so tried to ponder the facts as they wuz comin in. He tried to poke holes but Cassidy's story made sense. Finally, the lawman slapped his knee. Dam, I figured that boy wuz lyin to me. Im real sorry fer botherin ya like this. I'll have to check a thing or 2 up at the station, but I suspect we can close the file afterward. When Cassidy said adios and shut the door behind that lawman, he got to passin gas like thunder valley madness. Cassidy thought bout skippin town right then and there, but the boy pulled his boots up.

You see, there wuz just 1 thing that could prove or disprove Cassidy's story - the absence or presence of the dam bracelet's Yella ticket. If Freddie had snatched it off the counter like Cassidy said, it couldn't have been filed with the police. If the police did have a copy then surely Cassidy wuz the guilty inside man. Either way, someone wuz goin to the hoosgow!

As Cassidy watched that Detective walk back to his wagon with them silver bracelets danglin, hoowee did his legs get to movin. He burst up in the air, ran through the livin room an straight out the back winda. He had to get to the dam police station with the quickness! He jumped over the back fence and sped down the alley faster than a sneeze through a screen door. The kid crossed the street and spotted that Detective's car pullin out. He ran like the wind and crossed down to Sunset Road. Now, you may not remember none but when you wuz 21 you could do all types a superhuman feats. And when a feller is terrified of goin to the Hoosegow the mind gets focused with the quickness. You put them 2 together and that's dynamite! Cassidy wuz lit and pushed hisself like never before. He ran for his freedom through alleys, yards and cactus. He jumped stone walls and wood fences. He ran across the street into the police station parkin lot in record time. Any faster and he'd a-caught up to yesterday. Just as he wuz refillin his lungs he saw that Detective's car roundin the bend.

As luck would have it, good ole Roy wuz up front watchin Bonanza. Hi Roy, Cassidy said breathin like a mule. I want to see about gettin some hours. Roy looked him up and down. Dam boy, he said, why you so outta breath? Cassidy held his stomach real tight. You mind if I use the men's room real quick he asked em. Ah hell, go on boy Roy told em. Cassidy walked down the hall toward the toilet but darted over to that dam storage room when he saw Roy laughin at Hoss. He rummaged through boxes and bundles of Yella pawn slips. What month did Freedie pawn it? He wondered. Cassidy racked his brain.

Wyatt Erp once famously said, Fast is fine, but accuracy is everythang. He said, you must learn to be slow in a hurry. Never did an expression ring as true for Cassidy than at that moment. He calmed hisself. If the loan wuz gonna expire next week, then he did the math up in his head. February, he hollered to no one in particular. He searched the box slow in a hurry for the February bundle an by golly he found it. He flipped through the stack a Yella tickets. Guns, radios, speakers, VCRs. He wuz toward the end of the stack when he saw it. Freddie Kagen, Gold Nugget Bracelet, $2600. He ripped out the dang ticket, tossed the bundle back in the box and skedaddled.

He sprinted up the hallway just in time to see Detective So and So walk through the front door. Howdy Roy, I need to rummage through the pawn tickets the lawman said. Before the man spit his next word Cassidy bolted into the bathroom an lord almighty wuz his heart racin. There's only so much excitement a fella can take an Cassidy wuz nearin the end of his rope. Surrender had crossed his mind as he hid hisself in the last stall. All that regret washed down his guts and he felt like givin up right then and there.

Accordin to the Duke, courage is being scared to death, but saddlin up anyway. Well, it turns out Cassidy had an ounce a giddyup left. He put that Yella ticket in his mouth, chewed it up and swallowed it just as he heard the Detectives boots walkin by. Once he passed, Cassidy tiptoed back into the hallway. He stepped softer then a 2-minute egg to the front of that station and spoke to Roy in whispers. I'm hurtin' real bad he told em holdin his guts. I'm gonna call off doing them hours for now. Roy saw sweat pourin like a toad choker. Hell, son, I've been there once or twice myself Roy told em. Cassidy vamoosed and no one wuz none the wiser.

Cassidy kept his head down an worked hard, did his community hours, and golly did he git-er-done. Quick as a hiccup 3 months passed. He finished them community service hours and paid them court fines. He got released from probation and could get the hell outta Dodge.

An today, he wuz flyin out and leavin this here West Texas town in the dust. He'd lined up a little ole place and wuz headed to them sandy Florida beaches to live out his dreams under them palm trees sippin on pina coladas. That Ole Indian woman rode em to the airport, and he wuz grateful fer every dam thang she done fer em. She was sad to see him go but it was time to put out the fire and call in the dogs. Cassidy stepped to his gate, feelin some sorta relief that his young life might finally wind up on the right side of the Prickly Pear.

After that big ole jet airplane got to flyin, Cassidy pushed the seat back and put his eyes down below. He saw all them lowlifes and degenerates gettin smaller. He imagined all the scuz buckets and banditos, Columbian powder dealers and sniffers, all them nancy-boys, hoot owls an garden variety outlaws. The whole lot of em looked no bigger than a hill full of fire ants from way up yonder. He wondered what happened to Freddie Kagen and did Detective so and so send the poor bastard to the hoosegow.

He listened to the hummin of them jet engines and it got real quiet. Billowy puffs of clouds wuz whiskin and whirlin round while all the familiar shapes men see in their wakin hours began to dissolve. Cassidy could see past man's limited horizon for a hundred miles toward a purity unsullied by temptation and his own sinful proclivities.

The sun ignited the sky all ablaze, lightin up the plane's cabin ina bright orange glow. He could not be unmoved as his eyes took in the splendor of that glorious vision stretched out like a fiery path toward his destiny. God in heaven hardly ever allows a man to gaze into hisself with such clarity. Cassidy thought about all them terrible things he'd done, all them toad swindles, the burglerin, the stealin and the lyin. And especially the heartache he caused that Ole Indian women and even Freddie and Lucky too.

Cassidy's plane banked East and he starred out into the heavens. He watched the Texas sun dip below the mountains, castin long shadows over that dusty town. A truth set in an he wuz man enough to admit it. He wuz just another low-life degenerate no better than the rest of em. And right then and there he swore to the lord above that he'd get square with the world. Cassidy wuz gonna do right by every soul that crossed his path cuz that wuz like doin right by hisself. And with just a few minor indiscretions that aint even hardly worth a mention, that's just what Cassidy done! Vaya con dios, Amigo.

The Theatre of Magic

In a way that only happens when you're young and everything feels new, Nunzzos was where our lives started. Our sanctuary was constructed on the south side of the Seaside Heights boardwalk before we were even born. Nunzzos was a haven as unruly and vibrant as the lot of us, and as it changed, we did, too. This was no ordinary eatery; for decades, Nunzzos was a portal to nostalgia, its walls adorned with photos, posters, and memorabilia from the 40s and 50s, each piece transporting you to better times.

The air was thick with the aroma of simmering marinara sauce and freshly baked garlic bread, mingling with the buzz of arcade games and flickering pinball machines. As you walked inside, an electrifying charge filled the air, sending a tingling sensation through your fingertips with each step. The four of us spent our youth in that oasis. In fact, by the time I was 15, we'd become such fixtures that Mister Nunzzo hung a photo of us on the wall - just the four of us sitting on our bikes in the parking lot, holding up the man's famous pork roll hoagies. Mister Nunzzo even coined our gang's name. He called us the Pissers.

A few months ago, I drove past the boardwalk and felt an intense sense of belonging as I passed familiar intersections, buildings, and signs. Friends had told me what Nunzzos had become, but I was heartbroken to actually see it. A universal truth - nothing is forever, and that stings, doesn't it? Now, the restaurant's main building is a body piercing joint, and the arcade section was converted into a t-shirt and flip-flop shop, which had also gone defunct. The building's shell stood silent, its windows like the vacant eyes of an old man, staring blankly from the last chapter at the passing parade of life. Peeling paint and weathered walls covered in graffiti screamed abandon. As I watched younger generations walk past, I felt my heart break a little; they wouldn't know the name Nunzzos or experience that window in time. Arcade lights, music, and laughter that once echoed had now been replaced by an oppressive silence that lingered in my ear.

It wasn't just Nunzzos; the entire length of the boardwalk had been hallowed out. The carnival, the Ferris wheel, and the games of chance were gone; boarded-up buildings and vacant lots remained. It's strange to revisit a place you've not been in many years. You can walk there without an upward glance and yet see things unknown to most. It's the only time one's vision can permeate paint and wood and understand what's really inside, or at least what was. As I stood there staring, I could smell and hear what went on inside; the building itself was an old friend, its arms still open in a silent, reuniting embrace.

It's good to see you, old friend.

Yes, this was the place the four Pissers called home. I've known Jehovah Mike, Ira the Mensch, and Jimmy Red Pants since the first grade. My name is Sam, but they call me Sandman because "they claim" I'd fall asleep in class. Sure, like they were wide awake. When we weren't at school, we were on the boardwalk. Back then, it was a kaleidoscope of sights and sounds pulsating with a life all its own. It was a time when the world, teetering on the edge of a new millennium in the 80s and 90s, was brimming with unimaginable possibilities, plunged into the unabashedly loud and proud, and nowhere was this more apparent than on the boardwalk. It was a fantastical, neon-soaked Americana, the scene from a storybook vivant of summer's eternal promise where the ocean's roar competed with the shrieks of thrill-seekers and young lovers along with the unmistakable siren of laughter, music, and carnie barkers.

The air was heavy with the scent of fried foodstuffs – from clams to Oreos, a bonanza of artery-clogging delights. Thick, greasy smoke with aromas of sizzling sausages smothered in peppers and onions wafted through the air, colliding with the saccharine sweetness of cotton candy and buttery popcorn. The boardwalk was a vibrant marketplace of street foods, each stall a testament to America's melting pot ethos with a Jersey twist. And you hadn't lived until you'd sampled a Pork Roll Hoogie from Nunzzos. The pizza was as incredible as you'd get in Naples, and the gelato was as divine as in Florence.

The boardwalk was a place to learn about the world. We were local kids, shore rats, thronging the boardwalk, squealing after a particularly nauseating ride on the Tilt-A-Whirl, and discovering ourselves. Jehovah Mike was instrumental in teaching us to respect ourselves and to speak well of others. He wasn't religious. Mike is exactly the opposite of religious. He had no patience for hocus pocus, perhaps because his father was so intensely devout. Even as children, we could see it was foolish. We only called him Jehovah Mike because, on the weekends when we were kids, he'd walk up Vaughn Avenue with his dad, knocking on doors, handing out Watchtower Magazines, and talking about the end times. Jehovah Mike stuck out and the kid knew it. Mike was the only black kid in our class and the smartest kid in the whole dam school. He was thoughtful with his words, always looking, listening, and thinking; he had a natural wisdom that rubbed off.

The boardwalk gaming carnies called out to anyone walking by. *Step right up, and try your luck!* With their slicked-back hair and quick smiles, they lured in unsuspecting shoobies loaded with pocket cash. In fact, Ira's first job was just 2 blocks from Nunzzos at Banana Toes, a Meca for games of chance. He was sixteen and learned to entice passersby. *Knock down the milk bottles, pop the balloons, hook the ducks* – every win a triumph, every loss met with *better luck next time, pal!* Instead of suggesting they try again at half the price, Ira would confide, *Don't worry, no one ever wins.* Ira was an honest guy, too honest, and since he was Jewish, it was only natural we started calling him Ira the Mensh.

His Carnie career only lasted a week.

In the 90s, the Jersey Shore and boardwalks were more than just a destination; they were a cultural phenomenon, a microcosm of America at a crossroads. Bruce Springsteen, Bon Jovi, and Blues Traveler could be heard playing constantly - and band members would be seen sitting beachside just socializing or drinking an Orange Crush made with vodka, triple sec, orange juice, and Sprite. This was where nostalgia met the future, where tradition clashed and melded with the new. It was loud, brash, and smelled like funnel cake and hairspray. The nights were unapologetic – the clubs pulsated, and when Jehovah Mike hit the dance floor, he moved like no one we'd ever seen. When Mike moved in, others moved out, overcome with a sudden self-awareness that they looked silly in contrast.

As for Jimmy Red Pants - for years, we thought Jimmy might be on the spectrum. He was the sweetest and most pathetic little twerp. It was impossible not to follow him around to protect the kid. In the 3rd grade, he picked up the red puck from the urinal on a dare from Ned, the class bully. Everyone watched and laughed. Jimmy froze and stood staring while red liquid ran down his arm. Onlookers screamed and taunted him mercilessly. With an empty toilet paper roll next to the broken sink, he wiped his hands on his pants. That afternoon, the kid's transformation into Jimmy Red Pants could be corroborated by at least half the school.

In the 5th grade, Jimmy began to change. One afternoon on the playground, he predicted Jenny Carlsen would die in a fire. He pointed at her on the playground and stated his prediction matter-of-factly. It was spooky because his eyes widened, and his body shook. Two days later, in a drunken stupor, Jenny's father forgot about the Jiffy Pop burning on the stove. In those days, bay kitchens were designed with wooden dish cabinets suspended over the burners - not the most intelligent engineering. The rest of the family made it out in time, but Jenny was less fortunate. Ira and Mike passed off the tragedy as a coincidence until the morning of Tuesday, January 28th, 1986.

Our classroom was abuzz with excitement, a hive of young minds eagerly anticipating the marvel of human ingenuity - the launch of the Space Shuttle Challenger. Our 6th-grade class went giddy as Mister Abrahms rolled in the television so we could watch it live with the rest of the country. I noticed Jimmy shaking, and then he began whispering, which devolved into full-on shouting. He was frantic and couldn't stop pointing and yelling. Suddenly, the words coming out of his mouth registered. *The shuttle would explode.* He moved like a puppet fighting the puppeteer. Mister Abrams sat him down, got in his face, yelled, and made him shut up. Jimmy just sat there, staring wide-eyed as the voice on the T.V. counted down. *Four, three, two, one, and liftoff of the 25th space shuttle mission.* As the Challenger barreled into the sky, my fear that Jimmy was right subsided. It was a moment of pure, unbridled joy as we witnessed the culmination of mankind's dream to conquer the stars.

Then, the unimaginable happened. The Challenger erupted in a ball of fire, a bright, terrible blossom against a clear blue sky. The room plunged into a stunned silence, the kind that falls like a heavy shroud. "Obviously, a major malfunction," the announcer said. The air was thick with a collective loss of innocence, and the classroom transformed from a place of learning into the scene of an accident. Jimmy broke the morbid silence with a painful stab directed at mister Abrams. "I told ya it was gonna blow up," he shouted, wiping tears from his cheeks. Again, we brushed it off as a coincidence. It wasn't like rockets were safe or immune from exploding.

But we all understood that Jimmy's gift was both genuine and complicated. Ira, Mike, and I began to understand Jimmy possessed an eerie intuition that seemed to tug on him. He felt things and was pulled there mentally and sometimes physically. It's no wonder Jimmy Red Pants runs a hedge fund today. He has 200 employees, too. Bianchi Capital now manages billions for investors; his fund pays healthy returns, too. I even have a little in myself. Jimmy Red Pants has made a boatload of what he calls "Dough-Ray-Me." That spooky kid with red stains on his pants and a creepy intuition made a fortune. That little shit became a super generous man, a fantastic dad, and a doting husband.

Nowadays, the Pissers get together every year in mid-October. We stopped working, stopped raising families, and stepped off the hamster wheel for a 3 day weekend. We'll hit Vegas, Paris, wherever. Two years ago, Jimmy began constructing our dream getaway at the base of a mountain in Stratton, Vermont. I don't know where he got the idea - he has no connections to Vermont, none of us did. We affectionately coined it the Crimson Pants Lodge. We're talking 12,000 square feet, cedar beams, 4 stories, 7 bedrooms, 18-foot-high living room windows, a massive deck, fireplaces, a 25-person theatre, a jacuzzi, and a little shack for snowmobiles. Best of all, he added a custom addition just for the Pissers. He shared the blueprints over email a few times. And if you grew up in Seaside

Heights, you'd be excited, too. Jimmy spared no expense and built a replica of Nunzzos in the house, our home away from home, and the unveiling is today.

You should know that the boardwalk died after Sandy. Most places closed and never reopened. But Nunzzos held out. For years, it struggled but finally folded after Mister Nunzzo's murder in 2017. It was a horrific thing which rocked the community. Some men broke into Nunzzos after closing. Unfortunately for him, Lorenzo Nunzzo was in the back office doing some bookkeeping, and they shot him. The four of us were sick about it. Jimmy swore he'd find the men responsible. The community was shocked; everyone followed the case because Mister Nunzzo wasn't like family; he was our family. Days stretched to weeks, then months, but the police never found the 3 men who appeared in the pixilated camera footage. They were locals, and we know that because one of the men wore a Casino Pier hoodie. Mister Nunzzos' murder was the biggest reason Jimmy bought the house in Vermont. He kept saying it was about finding our getaway.

A few months after the murder, Nunzzos filed for bankruptcy. Jimmy followed the hearings for months, and after wading through years of New Jersey's bureaucracy, he finally bought everything at auction.

And by everything, I mean Jimmy got it all - every picture from every wall, all the tables and chairs, the video games, and the pinball machines, too. He bought the iconic sign out front and even the Nunzzos menu board that had hung over the counter. And it's all for us now, just 4 Jersey Shore rats. And who else besides the Pissers can keep Nunzzos' memory alive?

The four of us flew in this morning. Ira, Mike, and Jimmy got here earlier. As my cab descended The Crimson Pants Lodge's half-mile-long driveway, I rolled down the window and pushed my face out. Perhaps it was the trees or the mountains; no, it was the air. This Vermont atmosphere was not the sweltering air I was accustomed to. This mountain air was cool and thick, with a pine scent that permeated the nostrils. It filled my lungs with new hope so I could let go of work and responsibilities, become present, and be ready to enjoy what would surely be a momentous weekend. I hear gravel gently popping under the tires and see tall oak and birch trees forming an October canopy overhead. The light is easy here, but it may be my nostalgic state of mind that removes the strain. I saw a river of orange and yellow leaves floating above until the car came to a gentle stop.

When I stepped out, I was absolutely dumbfounded by the grandeur of this place. I'd only seen designs from emails Jimmy shared. This structure, reminiscent of a small lodge, was a hidden gem in the mountain's protective shadow. The massive wooden beams and intricate stonework harmonized with the vibrant autumn colors. Like Superman being drawn to his fortress of solitude, Jimmy Red Pants had surely been summoned here. It was nothing short of magnificent. The landscaping is immodest and impeccable, a lot like Jimmy is today. There's a grand lawn sporting symmetrically placed bushes and superbly stacked boulders near light-colored birch trees. I was drawn to the massive sideyard, which ends with towering trees at the foot of the forest. I rolled my eyes heavenward over the blanket of treetops, up over the mountaintop, and then to a crisp, luminous blue sky with a few white puffs perfectly suspended. *Glorious.*

The Crimson Pants Lodge will be our new hidden getaway, and it feels like a waking dream. I heard drum beats and immediately recognized the melody. I stood momentarily as the cab pulled away, taking it all in. As I step closer, 3 familiar faces wearing Cheshire smiles appear on the lemonade porch, moving to the drum beats like only shore rats can. This must be one of those special moments because the hairs on my arm stand at attention.

The music echoes, and seeing their faces takes me right

back.

But this house is haunted, and the ride gets rough; you've got to learn to live with what you can't rise above if you want to ride on down in through this tunnel of love.

I stood there, mesmerized as they closed the distance. It's only been a year, but reuniting with these 3 guys is like opening a cherished book you haven't read in ages, only to find its pages still brim with vivid tales and life's most important memories. "Step right up, Sandman, hook the duck or Shoot out the star; everyone's a winner," Ira barked. And I saw that skinny kid who used to steal wallets from under the towels of day-tripping shoobies. He was no thief. He ended up putting them back because he felt so guilty. Jimmy is twirling a rocks glass filled with amber liquid and twiddling a fat cigar. His friendly green eyes light up his face. "Call me when the shuttle lands," he says, shaking his head in disbelief. Then, like a game show host, Jehovah Mike announces the moment. "It's Seaside Heights hometown kid; he's your favorite and mine too – Sam the Sandman Allen." I move closer while Ira screams something about pork roll hoagies being stuck in my teeth since the 90s. We pat each other to make sure we're both real. "Why is there something and not just nothing?" Ira asks channeling Leibniz.

"I think, therefore, I am, and that's why I drove here," I reply with a grin. "Another year and you guys look about the same - magnificent."

"Another year, they sure fly by, don't they," Mike says as he hugs me. "Chuck Norris counted to infinity three times already," I shoot back. Mike went silent, and we beamed at each other. "Aren't you gonna kiss me?" he asks, and I'm unsure if he's kidding. "Look at you; have you been working out?" he asks. "You kidding me? Look at these guns." I say. "More like paper straws after 2 sips," he shoots back.

"Welcome to the Crimson Pants Lodge, Sam Sandman Allen," Jimmy announces as we give him our attention. "We are honored that you are here, and now the 4 Pissers have been reunited. Here's to good friends; tonight is kinda special, a little like one long night of mischief in A.C." He's preparing us for a Romanesque marathon of eating and drinking, which always takes place on the first night of reunification. The remaining days were strictly the recovery phase. "But we won't need a bail bondsman this time," I say. "Police, out here - Fuggetaboutit," Jimmy says, and I can't stop smiling. Jimmy pats me on the back. "Listen, Sandman," he confides. "Put your bag in a bedroom, pick any room not taken, and we'll meet you for…". He makes a rolling noise with his mouth and uses his hands to beat an imaginary drum set. "The grand reopening of Nunzzos!" Mike and Ira scream; Jimmy nods dramatically. "Oh, ya baby, oh yaaa, this is happening."

"You gonna paint the town red, Jimmy?" Ira asks. "Ba-da-pa," Jimmy retorts. Jimmy knows the extraordinary nature of the moment; we all did, and the excitement was thick.

As I walked up the stone pathway to the front porch, I was struck again by the immensity of this place, so I felt playful and channeled Thurston Howell. "Lovey, where do we keep the million-dollar bills?" I say. As I headed inside, I heard Ira yell back in his Lovey Howell impersonation. "They're in the same drawer as your erectile dysfunction medication, dear." I ignore him and head inside. After claiming a room and stashing my bag, I sprinted back down and spotted the bar. Within seconds, I'm pouring myself a Yamazaki 18-year-old, neat, with a couple cubes. I walk through the house, examining what I'd only seen in blueprints. Stunning, gorgeous, spacious, and elegant come to mind. It smelled of fresh paint, wood, metal, and leather. The views of the forest and mountains from the colossal living room are neither a foot nor an inch shy of breathtaking. *Nunzzos!* I knew where it was from the plans and couldn't wait for the others to join, so I headed toward the East wing through a large hallway and spotted the entrance.

I take in the iconic sign greeting me at the doorway. It's delicious to see but equally disorienting. I'd become familiar with the sign over decades. I only had to look up and see it perched on its 45-foot post outside Nunzzos, but it wasn't there anymore. Now, it was right here in front of me. *Nunzzos*. I reread it, studying the maroon cursive letters. Up close, you could see black shadows highlighting the red font, which I hadn't noticed before. I examined the patches of rust and ocean salt covering the metal brackets. I imagined how many people had put their eyes on this object over all those decades. The foyer was grand, but even so, the sign hardly fit, and I wondered how the contractors got it inside. When you have money, everything fits.

I hear the music spinning, so I step inside and see Nunzzos just like I remember, no better. Like a light bulb starting to glow, I feel adolescence rushing back. It's familiar and energizing. I scan dozens of framed paintings, photos, memorabilia, and posters on the walls. The wallpaper is, precisely as I remember, a blanket of black and white vintage newspaper ads that Jimmy had custom-made to match the sample he'd provided. I see photos of the Ferris wheel at Casino

The Theatre of Magic

Pier, the boardwalk, the state tourism posters, and the familiar faces of families eating and laughing. Then I spot the photo of the 4 Pissers sitting on our bikes, proudly holding our Nunzzo hoagies. That was 36 years ago, I thought. I move my eyes across the length of framed photos and posters lining the walls, and I know I'm home because the hair on my arms is levitating. "Call me when the shuttle lands," I say out loud, but I'm alone. Well, not entirely.

It was concentrated Deja vu when I spotted her. It was as if I'd stumbled across an object from another life, something I thought was a dream and lost forever. It was just a metal box, but this particular pinball machine is a relic of my youth - a testament to innocence and imagination. She's shiny and bright and staring back from the corner of the room. She flashes colors like a Bird of Paradise, tempting a new mate. A translucent blue and green light halo moves clockwise across the playing field. This was the original from Nunzzos, and it sparkled like a Christmas tree. I remember pumping in quarter after quarter. I'd listen as they fell into the slot, groaning and moving their way through the machine's internal workings, patiently waiting for the credit to register. But she didn't take quarters anymore.

I hit the start button, and the playfield lit up. It greets

me with its sinister and familiar voice.

Welcome to the Theatre of Magic.

In the playfield's center is a revolving magician's Trunk. If you can shoot the ball in, all hell breaks loose. Multiple balls appear from nowhere and start ricocheting around. More paddles come out, and a magnetic magician's ring causes the ball to levitate from one ramp to another. *Hokus Pokus*, it taunts. Toward the top, a strange-looking tiger holds a rotating buzz saw that starts spinning when you complete a feat. It wasn't just a game; it was a cruel jester, delighting in the players' despair, its laughter a chilling reminder that in this corner of the arcade, it wasn't just points being lost but a piece of the player's resolve, chipped away with each mocking laugh. *Who-ha-ha-ha-ha.* From the very first time I played, the movements were somehow familiar. *Hurry up*, it shouts. This metal box connects me to a higher realm within myself. I suppose that's why it's called The Theatre of Magic. *Shoot for the trap door.* The machine eliminates all those pesky laws of physics which constrain us out here. I know it sounds asinine, but it's as if this alien thing connects me to something I have yet to fully understand. It was right there, on the tip of my tongue, the edge of my mind; it felt inevitable, but it lingered there, just outside my grasp like a word I'd forgotten. Quetzalcoatl, Rumpelstiltskin, Rosebud! It tickled my thoughts, you know what I mean? I'd always felt that way. I didn't have much money back then, but Mister Nunnzo gave me all the quarters I needed to get my fill, and I'd play for hours. I can't believe it's here. I can't believe I'm standing in Nunnzos. The music is pumping, the lights are strobing, and the balls are bouncing.

"Remember when we lit you on fire?" Ira chirps from behind me. "I still have a mark on my shoulder, you bastards," I say without turning around. "That's a smallpox vaccination, you dingbat," he replies. He walks up beside me and pats me on the back. "Well, what do you think?" he asks. I turn my head and flash a smile that relays the level of my enthusiasm and the preposterous nature of his question, but I reply anyway. "Put it this way: I won't need any Viagra tonight, lovey!" Ira heehaws, then hijacks my right flipper. "Me neither," he claims while staring at the magician's spinning trunk. Then Ira pressed his hands together and kneeled before me like an Egyptian slave.

"A thousand pardons, master, for causing your immolation during that dangerous and naïve period known as youth." I wasn't sure if he was channeling David Carradine or Michael Caine. "Rise, oh great one, and man thy flipper," I reply in an equally confusing accent. "All is forgiven." Ira stood up and continued tapping without a strategy. He's always done that, and it didn't make sense because the ball was nowhere near his flipper. "Why use thy flipper when there is nothing when you can simply wait until there is something," I say, but he just keeps tapping. Lawyers require several fundamental talents, but pinball isn't one.

I'd always suspected Ira would become a lawyer. Sure, he was Jewish, so there was that, but that wasn't the whole story. His reasoning was flawless, and he could articulate multiple points of view even as a kid. All things considered, being an ambulance chaser made sense, too. If you knew Ira, you'd understand his propensity for patience, empathy, and justice, traits well suited for legal advocacy. He was a good guy despite doing the sleazy day-to-day work of chasing compensatory justice. He charged $750 an hour in lawsuits where the bulk of the work was photocopying evidence for the defendant's counsel. I used to work at a copy store, and we didn't charge $750 an hour. But in the end, he was doing right for people who'd been genuinely hurt. And he gave so much of it to the Boys and Girls Club; I loved that about him.

"A dumpster fire the world is," I say, channeling Yoda. "Viral pandemics, political and economic strife, climate change, resentment, A.I., war, human obsolescence -

it's madness out there." Ira taps his flipper and nods in agreement. He stares at the ball spinning around the magic Trunk. I can sense the wheels in his mind turning, too. "Now that I'm here, I think we should all move in," he tells me.

"I doubt my wife would get on board with that," Jimmy replies as he saunters in with Mike in tow. "Well, then she can stay at your apartment in N.Y.C.," I say. "I'm sure she'd prefer that to spending time with the Pissers." Jimmy nods while he bounces his head to the music, looking around. I can tell he's feeling rather proud of himself. Jimmy grabs the back of my neck. "Well, guys, what say you?" he asked, smiling so wide he could barely hold the cigar between his teeth. "It's a dream, Jimmy; I can't believe my eyes." I could hear our youth in each game's ding, ping, and whistle. A distinct melange of lights and sounds transporting us right back. We were together again, and the moment lingered deliciously. Without saying a word, and as we always had, we formed a circle, raised our glasses, and began shouting and gesticulating frantically to the music while guzzling scotch. For me, the first moments of being reunited were always magic. We played games, laughed, and danced around the newly reopened Nunzzos.

When we had our fill, we relocated to the sprawling

backyard deck. It was ideal for star gazing and taking in the mountain oxygen. "I want you to hear this, gents," Jimmy said as he swiveled his finger toward the audio system embedded in the wall. He tapped the screen, and a familiar synthetic beat repeated as the volume rose. "I remember this one," Mike shouted. "I REMEMBER, too," Jimmy replied, moving the volume past sanity toward adolescence.

Slowly, as if choreographed, Mike unwrapped a lovely tube of tenderloin and then opened the flaming grill. There was no questioning; he did the cooking when we were together. The music throbbed as the rhythmic chef inspected the peppercorns encrusting his prize. He grabbed a whisk and bowl of shiny liquid, spun it around, and poured the fluid across the now sizzling beef. Right on cue, Mike's engine roared, and we settled in to watch the show. Mike's movements can only be described as implausible, even unlikely. When the stars were aligned, and the music hit the correct sequence of tones, a new level was unlocked, and he'd be transported to another place, go limber, and fall into a trance. His arms, legs, and head began to channel bass, rhythm, and tempo. When Mike hit the clubs and moved across the dance floor in high school, time stopped, and the girls got wetter than an otter's pocket. Suddenly, a spatula appeared in one hand. He twirled it like a gymnast's ribbon, and I wondered if he'd been practicing this routine. He stepped and spun, kicked, and pointed.

Feeling the past moving in, letting a new day begin. Hold to the time that you know you don't have to move on to let go...

He floated headlong by the table, then levitated backward on full tilt. And Mike didn't need a partner – he slapped his own ass. He grabbed a bright orange oven mitt and pushed it down on one hand like the king of pop. His head flipped side to side while his body stayed motionless. Suddenly, he jumped up, landing in a full split. His body rose slowly without using his arms, and his muscles flexed. This was a spirit dance, a ritual summoning a call to war like a Haka dance without the chanting. In the distance, the deck's lights cast Mike's silhouette across the blanket of trees like a bat signal. He twirled like an ice skater as white smoke poured from the grill, enveloping his body. What a show. The 3 of us could only stare. "Call me when the shuttle lands," Jimmy declared while gurgling down more Yamazaki. As the music pumped, the Pissers moved with it.

It must have been Mike's performance, along with the $400 Japanese scotch molecules crossing our blood-brain barrier, that altered our collective state of mind. At that moment, I realized Ira was staring with a bedeviled expression. I followed his line of sight and landed on Jimmy's Glock 45, which sat shimmering in the middle of the table. Ira's eyes reflected the silver grip hypnotically, and I detected lost hope. Is that what Mike's dance had conjured? I realized our fortunes and futures now hung in the balance. The music was roaring, Mike was spinning, and I watched in horror as Ira reached out and snatched the Glock off the table. He slammed in the clip, then bolted down the steps into the sideyard. Jimmy yelled something and immediately took pursuit. I darted to the railing to see what was happening, and my body shook when I heard the gunshot ring out.

The boom echoed in the yard and off the mountain in the distance. As my field of vision cleared the railing, I watched Ira finish emptying the clip into a large birch tree. Each shot lit up his face, and he yelled "Yeee-Haaw" at the top of his lungs. Jimmy put his fingers in his mouth and sent a piercing whistle into the night sky, then he tossed Ira another clip and clapped for more. Our madness could only be described as an old West Jersey Shore house rave. Mike laughed hysterically. The music, the gunshots, the mayhem, the smell of tenderloin in my nose and scotch between my teeth. No mortal should feel this good. There goes the hair on my arms again. Um, bop, Um, pop. *I remember.*

We were loud and obnoxious, but the Crimson Pants Lodge sat on 93 acres. The only neighbor was a closed-down ski resort on the other side of the mountain. Past Jimmy's property, we were surrounded by Green Mountain National Forest and thousands of acres of unpopulated federal land. There wasn't anyone around to hear gunshots or pounding music, let alone call the cops on 4 drunk shore rats drenching each other in scotch and wailing like maniacs at the top of their lungs. We could do whatever we wanted out here. This was the genesis of Jimmy's idea.

Find your getaway.

When they stopped shooting that poor birch tree, we ate like Romans, which slowed us down. We complained about liberals and republicans, about the growing culture of grievance and the simmering anger that seemed to be building in everyone. We talked about the world's devolution. And it was unanimous: the world was doomed to repeat the same mistakes over and again for all eternity. We reminisced about the 90s and wondered if they could have been as fantastic as we remembered. We agreed that our life's window couldn't have been more perfectly timed. We talked about our jobs, families, and the death of empiricism. We called each other names and drank scotch till 3am. Correction: Ira didn't make it till 3. He passed out around 2, and Jimmy fell asleep in the hot tub wearing his birthday suit. Mike and I dragged him out so he wouldn't drown. It was his place, for Christ's sake.

Before I went upstairs, I pushed my drunken face to the sky and took in the concentrated stillness. My thoughts swirled in the wind amid the cold mountain air and below the wheeling bright glints of stars beyond the grasp of this contained little world where even the shortest distances are measured in light years. There was clarity in the sky and in each spec of light. The sky was crystalline. There was no surface light around here, so you could appreciate heaven's every detail. I can make out individual star clusters within our Milky Way, or were those just holes poked into the top of the jar so we don't suffocate?

As I fell asleep, I thought about my 4th-grade lunchbox, shaped like a farm. Inside was a thermos shaped like a corn silo. One afternoon, on the school bus home, Jimmy had to pee. His pleading got so bad that I relented, and he relieved himself in my beloved thermos. We did it discreetly at the back of the bus so no one noticed. I wanted to spare him the humiliation. Of course, I could never use it again, even if NASA had decontaminated the thing. I didn't care; Jimmy had become my friend, which was more important. For weeks, he thanked me. We developed a mutual trust after that. Sometimes, you can't know the value of a moment until it becomes a memory, and you can look back and understand what it meant. I collapsed into my bed and slept a deep, satisfying sleep.

I woke up hearing Mike and Jimmy singing. The smell of eggs, sausage, and hash browns filled the air. After moving downstairs, I spotted a pitcher of red liquid and knew the Bloody Marys were flowing. I proclaimed my disgust. "Liver health, gents." As our eyes met, Jimmy's grin widened. "The Sandman lives," he declared. "The Crimson Pants Lodge health department is mandating hair of the dog boosters for everyone."

"Do I have a choice?" I asked. Jimmy called my bluff and turned away with an exaggerated glum expression. "OK, OK," I relented. He scooped ice into a glass and filled the empty space with the red nectar. "What's with this mountain hike you've been selling us?" I asked. Jimmy held his hands up like a preacher and began his sermon. "Good people of Seaside Heights, today we make a pilgrimage on a journey of discovery." Mike and Ira immediately looked up from their plates with cynicism percolating. "First, we'll march up an old mountain trail," he roared. He used his hands to outline the path. "It's just past the property line and runs about 3 miles up and around the mountain. Then, we shall cross into the chosen land of Green Mountain National Forest. We'll continue up and around the mountain for another 2 miles." We listened to him speak from our hungover ears, and the mention of miles stirred anxiety in our throbbing heads. I wondered why we couldn't watch a movie, get in the hot tub, play more games, or shop in town. Why, in god's name, would we hike 5 miles hungover?

"That sounds... ambitious," I say to no one in particular. "Are we gonna make it?" I asked sincerely. Mike made his feelings known by channeling Kung Fu. "When you can walk the rice paper without tearing it after drinking Yamasaki all night, your DUI shall be expunged, Grasshopper." We all snickered, and our opposition to Jimmy's hike became clear. "I'll tell you why, Mike," Jimmy shot back. "We're a bunch of pudgy Keebler elves, and we need to move a little, for Christ's sake." Jimmy Red Pants was right about that. "You're all doing it, period," he demanded, and he slammed his fist on the counter. Wow, the Pisser was pissed, so we shut our mouths. Jimmy took in a deep breath and then calmly continued. "There's an old 1960s-era hippie commune. It's toward the top of the mountain, where we're headed. It's about a 90-minute hike. This will be something to remember, and you're all doing it; end of discussion."

We stayed silent. Jimmy had been texting and emailing about this hike for months. Why was he so deadset, I wondered? We had to sweat out the scotch, so I let it be. We finished breakfast, showered, shaved, and got dressed. I was the last one downstairs and spotted Jimmy stuffing energy bars, bottled water, and the Glock 45 into a backpack. The Pissers stepped off the back deck and started toward the mountain. As we walked, I spotted the carnage Ira inflicted on the birch tree. "Dam, Ira, you murdered it," I said as we passed the crime scene. Spent shell casings glittered in the grass amid splintered wood shards. "You're gonna plant 3 more now", Jimmy ordered.

The forest was majestic. White Pines and Cedars 80 or 90 feet high were perfectly spaced by nature. Life was everywhere. Birds, insects, moss on fallen trees. We spot intricate flowers and bright-colored mushrooms. The silence was cleansing, but a nagging question burned in my mind. "Why bring the Glock?" I asked. "Bears," Jimmy replied. "A few years back, some college kids spotted one, and instead of vamoosing, they pulled out their phones and started taking snapshots, snap chats, ticktocks, whatever they're called. The thing must have gotten territorial and charged them. The kids ran, but you can't outrun a full-grown black bear. When they re-grouped, one of the kids was missing. The bear got a hold of him and disemboweled him while he was still alive. The police went in and shot the bear, but the kid was dead. He'd been so badly mangled they had to keep the casket closed. I whistled the theme to Taps. "Not funny, Sam," Jimmy scolded. "Sorry, I'm just so hungover," I replied. After another minute, Jimmy continued. "The kid was maybe 19 or 20. Can you imagine how painful that would be? Man, what a way to go. So ya, I brought the Glock just in case." I wasn't a gun guy per se, but after hearing the bear story, I was glad Jimmy had it.

The Pissers came to a clearing and walked up a shallow creek. Water trickled over smooth, colorful stones lining the creek bed. After a while, we entered a clearing in the forest. Jimmy pointed to the ground. "OK, speaking of bears - take a gander, gents. That, my friends, is bear shit." We gathered around like you would in a game of three-card monte. As I examined the pile of excrement, I realized I'd never seen anything like it. "See the little red spots - those are berries.", Jimmy said like a college professor. "Those are tree and plant seeds that don't get digested." He jabbed a stick into the pile so we could see inside. "The scoop on bear shit is that each pile is a self-contained, ready-to-grow plant - complete with deshelled seeds surrounded by a fertilizer base so the seed can begin growing. It's almost as if the plants create fruit to attract bears." Our hedge fund guy must be a part-time botanist.

"Free fecal freight," Ira shouted. "Deshelled Dung delivery," Mike fired back. "Poop propagation pods," Ira returned fire. "Excrement-encased embryos," I said. "Seed Scattered Scat," Ira Replied. "Ok, please, guys," Jimmy demanded and was grateful he did.

We followed the creek without speaking. The sounds of our footsteps became rhythmic, and perspiration formed on my temples. Dashes of sunlight filtered through a cathedral of leaves, and the forest's silence echoed even with the rustling leaves. The canopy of branches and leaves seemed to hold us in. It was easier that way, and I allowed my eyes to wander over the details of each tree. Each gnarled Trunk told a tale not unlike the chapters of life. The mighty Eastern Cottonwood and Silver Maples stand as testaments to resilience, their roots delving deep into the mysteries of the earth, holding secrets in their silent vigil. And in the inevitable fall of the old, lying moss-covered and surrendering to the forest floor, there is a dignified end – a final chapter that nourishes the next generation, ensuring that in death, as in life, there is beauty, purpose, and a continuity that transcends the individual. Here, life's chapters were laid out plainly without exaggeration or drama. I couldn't help but think we were destined to be here, and I was grateful Jimmy pushed us.

We passed through a ravine and saw 5 abandoned cars. There were no roads, so I wondered how they got in there. It was apparent they'd been sitting for decades. We peeked inside a rusted Ford Thunderbird and a Chevrolet Bel Air whose interior was mint green. The windows were gone, and the exteriors were in their final state of dilapidation. There were hundreds of bullet holes in the bodies. Jimmy pointed to a smiley face shot in the quarter panel. If you've never encountered someone's target practice, you've never been on an actual hike.

After another 20 minutes, we stopped to examine a small pond. It was runoff from the mountain peak. We were 80 percent to the top of the mountain. I noticed Jimmy's hands began to shake. "You ok?" I asked, but he didn't answer. His breathing quickened, and his eyes locked onto something in the distance. I spotted something manmade and pointed. "There's something past those trees." We stared for a moment, then moved closer. As we got near, I realized it was a mobile trailer - white with blue trim. It was similar to one you might see at a construction site used as the foreman's office. The frame was small, with a front door and a window on the side. A large metal chimney stuck out from the roof with reams of haphazardly placed duct tape holding it in place. Dual wheels held up the back while wooden blocks propped up the front. An industrial-sized propane tank sat just next to it. It seemed out of place for a lot of reasons.

I walked around the back and saw hundreds of metallic wrappers littering the ground. Clearly, the proprietors were not environmentalists. Dozens of cardboard boxes lay stacked on one side of the trailer. Printed on the boxes was the familiar Johnson & Johnson label. As Mike peered into the trailer's window, I lifted a box resting on a green plastic barrel. I saw hundreds of discarded Sudafed packets. "There's 3 ovens inside and glass beakers everywhere", Mike reported. Jimmy approached me and pointed to a box filled with empty bottles of nail polish remover. He looked over and raised his eyebrows. "I'm, Imma, I'm getting a weird feeling," his voice cracked.

There was an uncomfortable silence, but I didn't understand why. "Jimmy, what is this?" I asked. "It's a meth lab, Sam, so please, let's go now," Mike said without making eye contact. There was a moment of shock when the tone in Mike's voice registered over Jimmy's silence. Without another word, we began walking briskly back towards the small pond. All sorts of thoughts swirled in my head. Drug dealers, chemists, and what an ingenious place to put a meth lab – or maybe not.

A man's voice shattered the forest's silence in a painful rip. "What are you doing here?" the voice demanded from behind us. The stranger's voice injected 2 cups of pure alarm into my gut. The Pissers spun around. I saw a man walking toward us, and he was holding a long gun. He was tall but not very muscular. His face was red and bloated, and his eyes were black as obsidian. His buzz cut was entirely out of place, and there were red marks down the side of his head, perhaps where a clipper left its tracks. He wore a light green jacket and dark jeans. A gigantic silver belt buckle glimmered where his Jacket opened, and the man stepped toward us.

Jimmy calmly raised his hands, showing the stranger his palms. "Nothing at all", he replied calmly. "We're just hiking." Mike, Ira, and I held our hands out casually to mimic Jimmy's gesture. "I saw you looking inside the trailer – What were you looking at?" the man asked. His voice shook and rang of ignorance, which was terrifying. "Nothing in particular," Jimmy admitted. "We're just hiking up the mountain - headed to the old hippie commune." The man stepped closer to examine us, his eyes unforgiving, and his mouth twitched like an angry dog. "We aren't armed or anything," Jimmy declared. My mind immediately went to the Glock in his backpack. *Please, God, don't let anything happen.* Isn't it amazing how we can beg God for help in our most desperate hour and then ignore the payback we promised when we're out of the woods? Pun Intended. I swore I wouldn't do that if God would save us now.

I was accepting of the man's assault rifle because even though it was pointed in our general direction, the barrel was tilted down. A military-style ammunition clip protruded at the bottom. Then I spotted the man's footwear and knew we'd stepped in it. I stared at the man's brand-spanking-new blue python cowboy boots, and they stuck out like a bikini-clad woman delivering a church eulogy. His boots weren't just blue; they were baby blue. The forest was no place for $3000 show boots. Combine that with the dude's bizarre buzz cut, those red blotches, that belt buckle, and the assault rifle - don't forget the meth lab. This man was a drug dealer, the real McCoy, too. "What were you guys looking for?" the man asked again.

Jimmy smiled. "Nothing really; we thought the trailer was abandoned. We saw some old, abandoned cars just down the hill. Hey, man, we didn't take anything; we're just hiking." A staticky voice exploded from the man's Jacket. "Diego, did you stop them? What's happening?" the voice demanded. The man retrieved an expensive-looking walkie-talkie. "Ya, I got 'em ere. There are four of em, and they say they was hikin. One was lookin in da window, and they was nosin around ina trash."

"Don't do anything to em until we get there," the voice ordered.

"Ya, OK," the man said, then stuffed the walkie-talkie back in his jacket pocket. "Look, sir...it's Diego, right?" Jimmy asked, but the man didn't respond. "Look, Diego, we are family men and don't want any trouble. We didn't see anything; we don't want anything, and we're gonna get out of your hair and leave you in peace." Jimmy began walking backward. "Wait for my friends," the man ordered. "They want to talk to you." Jimmy continued to back up. The Pissers began walking backward. Ira's hands shook like leaves in a hurricane. The man lifted the assault rifle and pointed it squarely at Jimmy. "I said wait fucker", he shouted. "OK, calm down", Jimmy replied. "Get on your knees," the man ordered. Ira closed his eyes and swallowed a tennis ball. My vision blurred, and my heart pounded in my neck. The Pissers did what they were told and got on their knees. We stared at the stranger who was now holding us hostage at gunpoint.

Don't do anything to em until we get there.

I analyzed that phrase repeatedly as we kneeled quietly, listening to the subtle sounds of nature, waiting for some unknown fate while staring at the stranger wearing baby-blue python cowboy boots and holding a rifle. Diego was a nice guy's name, I thought. I thought about all the Diegos I'd known but couldn't think of any. Besides, what meaning can be derived from a name alone? Does someone's name influence who they become? That was a decent question, but I realized this wasn't the time or place to ruminate. "We didn't see anything," I declared without thinking. "What would there be to see?" Diego asked snidely. "I dunno," I replied as innocently as I could. "Cool boots," I said, realizing how stupid I must sound. God, was I hungover. Jimmy shot me a firey look that was crystal clear: SHUT UP! Diego looked us over; his eyes moved fast, and his chin and lips twitched like he'd been on a 3-day bender.

Jimmy's eyes were wide and dark; they didn't blink and spoke to us silently. Mike let out a cough, then another. He held his hands to his mouth as he coughed, and then he began gagging. "I'm sorry," he pleaded. "I'm hungover and dehydrated, and the site of guns makes me nervous. I have a heart condition." For a second, I wondered if Jehovah Mike had been remiss in disclosing some ailment, then realized he was putting on a show for the end times. He continued coughing and gagging so forcefully that a good amount of bloody vomit came up. *Thank God for the Bloody Marys.* Diego winced. *Superb theatre.* "Jimmy, a bottle of water, please," Mike begged as he allowed vomit to dangle from his lips dramatically. Having known him for almost 40 years, I could tell it was spurious, but to an outsider, it appeared genuine. "Can I at least give him water?" Jimmy asked, pointing to the pack on his back. The man stared as Mike coughed and gagged. "Ya ok."

Using his right hand, Jimmy slowly reached around his head, unzipping the backpack. He retrieved a water bottle and tossed it to Mike, who opened it quickly and put it in his mouth. Frantically, he chugged it, and water flowed generously down his neck and chest. He appeared to be declining fast. *And the Academy Award goes to.* Mike caught his breath. "Thank you, sir," he said, bowing subserviently, which was surreal. Diego nodded. "Thank you, sir," Jimmy echoed. Diego nodded. "Could I have water, too?" Ira asked instinctively, holding his hands together like he was in church. Now, he was acting, playing the battered housewife. "I have more bottles here," Jimmy admitted. Diego nodded a third time. "Ya, ok."

Jimmy moved his hand behind his head again. Like a magician, his hand appeared with another water bottle. He handed it to Ira, who guzzled it like he'd crawled through the Sahara Desert. "Sorry about that, sir. We were drinking Japanese scotch last night, and we got really hammered." Diego nodded. "The good stuff," he said with a smirk. Can you build a rapport with your captor? Jimmy peered into me, and I understood the instruction. We had to get to the bottom of his backpack. "I'm thirsty too," I pushed out in a cracked voice. "Could I have water?"

"Enough with the wooder," the man said with an accent that popped in my ear. Not because it was unfamiliar but because I was all too familiar. It was a common mispronunciation among the toothless types back at the Shore. Diego was getting annoyed, and I sensed there was little rope left. Jimmy's dark eyes screamed at me. It was now or never, so I improvised. "Oh, please, I have the diabetes," I begged, thinking it might be a disease that required large quantities of water. I could see Jimmy wanted to smack me. "Diego, we're coming up the ridge," the voice on the walkie-talkie roared, and a vehicle's engine revved in the distance.

Jimmy's eyes caught mine. He needed an excuse to go into the backpack. The hairs on my arms were going up. "Please, Jimmy, I need water; please give me water," I begged. "He does have diabetes," Jimmy confided, and I could see Jimmy's hands shaking like the day the shuttle blew up. "Let me give him water." Jimmy reached back without getting permission. "Christ, give 'em a wooder then," the meth head relented. Jimmy retrieved the Glock, which appeared like a magic trick in his hand. In the blink of an eye, the gun was cocked and aimed. I saw Diego's eyes grow wider. As Gomer Pyle used to say - Surprise, Surprise, Surprise. "Shoot!" I began to yell, sensing the man's assault rifle about to pivot. But Jimmy's senses were faster. *Pop, Pop, Pop.*

The expression on the stranger's face instantly changed. I saw disappointment register as he fell backward, realizing how quickly the tides could turn. "Oh god, no," Jimmy yelled, then jumped up and grabbed the man's rifle as we watched him wheeze and cough up blood. I felt the urge to help him. We watched for a few seconds until he stopped moving. In the distance, we saw a black Range Rover pull into the trailer's encampment. The 2 men inside easily saw Jimmy gun down Diego. As soon as they jumped out, gunshots rang out from across the clearing, and we were now being shot at by Diego's buddies. I could feel the buzz in the air each time a bullet whizzed by. We darted behind a large tree. Jimmy tossed the Glock and his backpack to Ira. "There's 3 more clips in there."

"This is live or die, so get your mind in the game," Jimmy demanded as he studied the 2 men in the distance. Jimmy fired a few shots from Diego's rifle while Ira reloaded the Glock. *Pop, Pop, Pop.* "I see two men 150 feet ahead; one's wearing a brown jacket, and the other's jacket is orange", Jimmy reported as he peered around a tree trunk. *Pop, Pop, Pop.* Jimmy's eyes lit up. "I'm gonna shoot the propane tank," he declared. "They're nowhere near it," Ira shouted. "They want to keep this place a secret, don't they?" Jimmy replied frantically. "That's the only thought going through their heads right now. If we can make the tank explode, then someone may see it. More importantly, those guys will think their cover is blown when others come up here to investigate. That means they'll leave us be. So, cover me, Ira." Ira nodded in agreement.

Jimmy's hands were still shaking, but he got up on one knee, aimed, and pulled the trigger. *Pop, Pop, Pop.* "Nothing", he said. Jimmy stood up entirely and carefully aimed at the tank. *Pop, Pop, Pop.* "It's not exploding," he said desperately. *Pop, Pop, Pop.* "It's not exploding," he shouted in frustration. He tried again. *Pop, Pop, BOOOOM.*

I maneuvered my head around the tree and watched a fireball erupt over the propane tank. The trailer immediately burst into flames, as did surrounding trees. Fire and thick black smoke rose through the treetops. We were nearly at the top of a mountain; surely, the fireball and smoke would be seen for miles. But would anyone come in time? Another loud blast sounded and tore the trailer to bits. A voice crackled over the walkie-talkie in Diego's jacket. "If you've hurt my brother, If you've hurt my brother," a man's voice screamed with hysteria. We stared at Diego's lifeless body; his baby blue python boots were pointing to heaven. The walkie-talkie crackled static, then went silent.

Jimmy studied the men's position and then knelt down. "OK, Mike and I will flank, right," he said. "Ira and Sam, you flank left. You guys move around the camp clockwise to the other end and try to hold their attention while we get closer. When we get over there, Ira – You gotta take them out from behind." It was apparent Jimmy's senses were pulsing, so we trusted his instruction. What else could 4 shore rats do in a moment like this? I have to admit, to be drenched in adrenalin was an absolute delight. I was wide awake and living in the now. And it was indisputable - I was scared out of my gourd, but the hangover was gone. The pine-filled air filled my lungs, and I took it in while bullets whizzed past. The air must have been laced with helium because I began to feel much lighter.

As Ira and I ran from tree to tree, I saw blue and orange lights blinking throughout the forest. It might be an ambulance or a police car. No, I was having a panic-induced hallucination. Jimmy darted from tree to tree, moving further away. Mike followed. I watched the two until they vanished behind a patch of fallen trees.

I heard my pinball game laughing at me from behind a tree. *Whooo hahaha.* Something is happening. I heard gunfire, but the bullets weren't whizzing by us anymore. They must be shooting at Jimmy and Mike. I pushed my head up enough to see the 2 strangers. The leafy canopy refracted the voices and gunshots, which lingered in midair like the percussiveness of thunder. The empty pit in my stomach called my eyes to scan farther, and low and behold, I spotted her under the trees in the distance.

My pinball game was out here, in the middle of the forest. It must have followed me. Its lights blinked brightly, and it laughed and called out. I began moving toward it in a considerable state of disorientation. "Where you going? Don't leave," Ira begged. I moved closer, and the closer I got, the better I felt. I heard the guys screaming at me, but I smelled Marinara sauce and Garlic bread. "Save Ira," I heard Jimmy shout. I turned my head to see what all the commotion was about. I noticed that the man in the orange Jacket was closer to Ira, who was now hunched down. As I took in the scene, It was evident that Ira's spirit had withered, and he sat cowering behind a tree.

I snapped out of it. "Ira, he's running toward you!" I yelled, but I was 100 feet away now. Ira looked up, and I saw terror on his face. Ira dropped Jimmy's Glock and covered his ears. "Sandman," Jimmy pleaded in the distance. I must have reached outer space because the air evaporated, time stopped, and my arms began to rise. All I could think about was Mister Nunnzo smiling while he filled my hands with quarters. "It's time to play", he said. I saw the Ferris wheel turning at Casino Pier and heard the familiar voice again. *Welcome to the Theatre of Magic.* A halo of translucent blue and green lights bursts out between white flashes, rotating across my field of vision. Ira became the magician's Trunk, and while I wasn't sure I was completely lucid, I felt utterly alive. *Shoot for the Trunk*, the game taunted.

As I ran toward Ira, I noticed my feet were no longer

touching the ground. I was higher now, floating, no flying but running, too. Surely, this was a dream. I saw Jimmy and Mike stand up from their crouching position and stare in disbelief. I darted in between trees as the man stepped closer to Ira. I noticed the other stranger in the brown jacket staring at me, his jaw gaping. He took a few shots, but I was too fast. As I moved in, the man rounded the tree and found Ira quivering. "You shot Diego," he screamed as he raised his rifle. *Hurry up.* Ira looked up at the man, and time stopped.

I swept my hand across the ground and retrieved a large, smooth rock. The forest was frozen. As I came into range, the man looked up, and for a moment, sheer terror lingered in his eyes. I swung the rock and felt the man's tissue and skull give way to its mass and momentum. Scalp, bone, and brain fragments spread through the air. I watched the pink mist expand outward. I floated there, pondering physics as seconds stretched minutes. The man's blood sprayed across Ira's face while his body exploded backward. The stranger wasn't riding a roller coaster, but the expression on his face was close enough. This was intoxicating, and I allowed myself to rise higher toward the treetops. *You have the magic, who-ha-ha-ha.* In the distance, I saw Jimmy and Mike frozen, staring, and something roared past my ear, perhaps a 3-pound mosquito. A few more whizzed by, and then I felt a blow to my left shoulder and lost my ability to float.

I saw the 3rd man sprinting closer as I fell through the air. He pushed out a gut-curdling scream as bullets sprayed from his rifle. When I hit the ground, I turned my head up and stared at the man hovering over me. I took in the details of his face as he lifted his rifle. More shots rang out. *Pop, Pop, Pop.* The man turned just in time to watch Jimmy Red Pants empty Diego's clip into his chest. He was dead before he hit the ground. Sunlight flashed through the canopy overhead, and I heard Mike screaming my name. Everything got bright, and I knew it was going unconscious.

When I came around, I smelled burning chemicals. The forest was calm and silent now. I saw the propane tank flaming and what was left of the trailer. Thick black smoke filled the air, and 3 familiar faces towered over me. None of them wore Cheshire smiles. My left shoulder was bloody and throbbing. Someone had ripped my shirt sleeve and tied it around the wound. "You're OK, Sandman," Jimmy said softly. "The bullet grazed your arm." Everything felt normal again except the way the Pissers stared.

"Sam, what just happened?" Jimmy asked firmly. I sat up, and my 3 friends began interrogating me. "How did you do that?" Ira asked, looking me up and down. "How did you move like that?" Mike demanded. "You were floating, Sandman." I pushed out an answer. "I dunno, something lifted me up," I said. "Are we hallucinating?" Ira asked. "How could you float like that?" Mike demanded. "Let him breathe," Jimmy shouted. "I don't know what happened," I screamed. "I was scared, and something moved me like a puppet," I said. "I felt like a puppet." The Pissers appeared unconvinced. "Maybe it was a hallucination, that meth lab, the chemicals, I dunno."

Jimmy looked at Mike, who looked at Ira. "4 people can't share the same hallucination", Jimmy deduced. "Look, someone probably saw the explosion, and they'll be up here to investigate. The question is, do we want to be here to explain this?" We talked about staying and admitting our role. We debated the merits and drawbacks. Would the police or a prosecutor believe an unbelievable tale? We had to consider ourselves and our families.

We discussed what to do with the bodies. Jimmy thought we should retrieve the slugs from Diego's torso, but no one volunteered to play surgeon. It wouldn't matter if they didn't have the gun, so we'd have to ditch it. "It's obvious from the scene that a last man is standing," Mike declared, taking inventory.

"Wipe our prints off their rifle," Jimmy said. "This is a simple drug partnership gone sour." Jimmy thought for a moment, then dragged the 2nd man's body closer and placed the bloody rock in his palm. He returned Diego's gun, staging it next to his outstretched hand. Using a leafy branch, he wiped the drag marks and footprints from the ground.

I followed the Pissers on the hike back, keeping my distance. When we got close to the edge of Jimmy's property, he asked us to take our shoes off and walk the rest of the way in our socks. "Don't leave any footprints," he demanded. "Stay on the thickest parts of the grass," he ordered. When we arrived at the house, Jimmy collected our shoes, boots, and my bloodied shirt and threw them in the wood pile. We watched him douse the pile with gas, and then he lit a match. *Woosh.*

We stripped so Jimmy could wash our clothes. I showered, and Ira bandaged me up. I had saved his life. We sipped scotch and stared into the roaring fireplace. Not a word was spoken. Jimmy switched on the evening news toward the night's end, but nothing about our eventful afternoon was reported. We debated leaving the following day, but Ira argued that we couldn't change our flights because that would destroy us in court. "Everything has to stay the same," he kept saying.

On Sunday, we watched movies all day, never leaving the house. The guys spent some time in Nunzzos playing games, but I was too scared. I could hear the game's voice laughing and felt myself floating. *Welcome to the Theatre of Magic.* I was terrorized at the thought of what might happen if I saw her. Finally, the day ended.

On Monday morning, we ate breakfast on the back deck. We'd be heading to the airport in 2 hours. My shoulder was throbbing, but the sharp pain was gone. Mike turned on some music, and the mood lightened. Our appetites were back, and we ate quietly, only glancing up the mountain a few times, wondering exactly what we'd experienced. As we were clearing the table, we heard vehicles approaching. The Pissers watched in horror as 2 police cars crept down the long driveway and stopped in front of the house. "Just as we talked about," Jimmy said. "We have not left the house since arriving." We all nodded. "We had to take the stupid hike," Mike murmured aggressively. "Shut up!" Jimmy ordered.

Casually, Jimmy walked down the back steps toward the driveway. The 3 of us moved to the railing. Four uniformed policemen emerged from the cars and began walking toward us. "Morning," Jimmy said, greeting the men. "Morning," a tall, uniformed cop replied. "Are you the homeowner?" he asked. "Yes, I am," Jimmy admitted. "Your name is Jimmy..." the cop lingered, looking at a notepad. "Jimmy Bianchi, the one and only," Jimmy replied playfully. "And you are?" The cop looked up toward the deck and took inventory, glancing around for anything out of place. "Mister Bianchi, my name is Constable Boomer Walker with the Stratton Police Department." His brown eyes were sharp and unwavering. The man's face and build communicated an acumen for police work and an authority not to be trifled with. "We're investigating an incident which occurred just a few miles from here."

"OK, how can I help?" Jimmy asked innocently. "Have you been in the woods this weekend?" the man asked. Jimmy shook his head. "We have not been in the woods," he replied without wavering. "We've been inside, eating, drinking Japanese scotch, playing games, and watching cheesy movies." Jimmy knew that small details painted big pictures. "What are you investigating," Jimmy asked like any concerned homeowner would.

"Three men were killed, shot, on the mountain."

Jimmy looked at the man without blinking. "That's

horrible," he said. "We've been here all morning and have not seen anything."

"We believe the incident occurred on Saturday afternoon," the cop said, staring at Jimmy's flip-flops. "When was the last time you left the property," he asked. "We've all been here since we flew in on Friday morning. We haven't seen or heard anything since we got here." The constable looked toward us and waited for a confirmation, so I spoke. "I haven't seen or heard anything since we got here." Ira and Mike shrugged and replied with the same useless answer. "Did any of you hear an explosion or see smoke on the mountain?" he asked. We all shrugged. "I'm sorry, but we've been inside all weekend," Jimmy replied. "Can I ask who was killed? I mean, shootings, explosions, smoke, what happened exactly?" Jimmy asked, keeping himself in character.

The man bounced his head from one side to the other. "Three men were killed, two of them shot, one of them bludgeoned," he replied, closing his notepad. "They were cooking crystal meth in a makeshift lab tucked away up the mountain. It seems they were producing it here but distributing in New Jersey." No sooner had the words come out of the man's mouth than a knot formed in my gut. Ira turned and looked at me. "Two of them have lengthy criminal records, burglary, distribution of a controlled substance, assault, and one of them is a suspect in a robbery and homicide from 2017." The cop could see his onlookers were in genuine shock. "Put it this way," he continued. "It's fortunate you stayed inside."

"Jesus," Jimmy replied, now actually reeling. "This is not the community news we were hoping for." Jimmy looked at the other officers.

"It's a shock to us, too - we don't get a lot of bad guys around here," the cop remarked as he scanned the yard. "It's just the four of you at the house?" he asked. "Just the four of us," Jimmy said firmly. "It's simply magic," the cop remarked. "Excuse me," Jimmy shot back. "This place, it's simply magic," the cop said as he inspected the Crimson Pants Lodge. "I remember it being built. I'd spot trucks and equipment pulling in here for months."

As the man spoke, I noticed him glancing toward the birch tree that Ira had shot up in his drunken stupor. There were clearly visible bullet holes blasted in the Trunk, and a fresh pile of light-colored wood chards littered the grass below. If the man was 10 feet closer, he'd easily spot a couple dozen bullet casings littering the ground. And in that instant, I realized that the slugs in the tree, if retrieved, would perfectly match those lodged in our friend Diego, the dead guy wearing baby blue python cowboy boots.

"Thank you," Jimmy replied, his voice cracking. "We love the solitude and are grateful to be part of the community. We love cooking out and making new friends, and we'd be happy to have you fellas over for a steak and beer. I am sorry we can't be much help today". The cops' eyes seemed to lock onto the bullet-ridden birch tree. "I've heard meth can make men do terrible things," Jimmy said, quickly re-engaging the constable. "There's one thing I've learned in my life." Jimmy stared down the man, and there was an uncomfortable silence. "What's that?" the man asked. "No one escapes their deeds," Jimmy replied soberly. "It sounds like those men got exactly what was coming." The cop smirked, pushing the notepad into his jacket pocket. "You're probably right," he replied. After filling his lungs with a deep gulp of mountain air, the cop nodded. "Have a nice day, mister Bianchi." The man lifted his open palm toward us, and then the 4 cops returned to their cars, and we watched them drive away.

Jimmy turned and faced us. "Distributing in New Jersey," he repeated. "A suspect in a homicide from 2017. And you, Sandman. What in the hell is happening here?" I didn't know what to say. "Were those the guys who killed Mister Nunzzo?" Mike asked, but all of us already knew the answer. "But how?" Jimmy asked. "What is this, Sam?" Mike demanded. "What are the odds we'd cross paths with Mister Nunzzos' killers on some random mountain?" My thoughts scrambled for an answer, which hád been there all along. "The tourism poster," I shouted. "What poster?" Ira asked, but I'd already started running.

I sprinted inside the Crimson Pants Lodge toward Nunzzos, and the Pissers followed. I lifted my eyes as I entered, scanning dozens of framed posters and photos covering the walls. "Did the contractors put up everything like it used to be?" I asked. "Yes, exactly like it was," Jimmy replied. I walked the length of the far wall, looking over familiar memorabilia until I spotted it.

In the twilight of the arcade-lit room, our eyes locked onto a framed poster that had adorned the walls of Nunzzos for decades. It was an innocuous thing, a relic of a forgotten era. Its paper edges frayed inside the frame, and monotone colors faded by the relentless march of time. Yet, in the eerie glow of arcade lights, the image and words beamed with the surreal message we'd seen 1000 times before. It was a simple drawing of a mountain range with 2 distinct peaks, identical to the 2 peaks seen outside the window. I read the block of text out loud.

Stratton Vermont, find your getaway.

There it was - a simple suggestion. A seed planted decades ago, which lay dormant. And it became clear that Jimmy's mind wasn't the only place where the seed had taken root. The 3 men had been regulars at Nunzzos too. *Stratton, Vermont, find your getaway.* We stared at the poster, and the power of karma couldn't be more evident. I glanced at a nearby photo of Mister Nunzzo. He was smiling, almost glowing, his grin more profound, and in his eyes, I saw acceptance. My jaw shook. A tear ran down my cheek. There goes the hair on my arms again.

We flew home and went back to our lives. Each of us lived in fear that police might burst in, serving arrest warrants for murder. Days turned into weeks, then months. Yes, our illusion about the world had been lifted. It sounds bizarre to speak the words, but an invisible force watches us, and it's as powerful as gravity. It counts the deeds that percolate from us throughout our lives like the slow drip of a rusty, forgotten faucet. You wouldn't be able to label it good or bad; it's not that simple; it's more like a director on a stage where actors get nudged when they deviate from what's expected.

The parts of my life that have made the most sense are the most difficult to describe using words. I see a movie playing in my head. The reel features the faces of the people I've loved against the scenery of the places I've lived. The curtain opens, and suddenly, there they are. And I sense that invisible force watching like a protective mother. I might be listening to the rain, staring out the window, or waiting for a traffic light to turn green, and there it is. It's quietly planning an end to one chapter and the beginning of another. You can see and hear it if you listen and watch. It will sound and look differently to every ear and eye. Still, it's well-hidden, only recognizable by the keenest of observers. We get what we give; there are no exceptions, and when we keep our imaginations alive and open our hearts, if we allow ourselves to see the extraordinary in the ordinary, we become a doorway to the theatre of magic.

The Theatre of Magic

THE THEATRE OF MAGIC
AND OTHER STORIES
RAFAEL COSENTINO

Milton Keynes UK
Ingram Content Group UK Ltd.
UKHW021632040624
443725UK00029B/313